POINTBLANK

OTHER BOOKS IN THE EXTREME FICTION SERIES

Book 2: *Breakout*
Book 3: *Real*

POINTBLANK

MARK A. REMPEL

Publishers Since 1798

THOMAS NELSON PUBLISHERS®
Nashville

A Division of Thomas Nelson, Inc.
www.ThomasNelson.com

Copyright © 2002 by Mark A. Rempel

Published in Nashville, Tennessee, by Thomas Nelson, Inc.

Scripture quotations are from THE NEW KING JAMES
VERSION. Copyright © 1979, 1980, 1982, Thomas Nelson, Inc.,
Publishers.

Library of Congress Cataloging-in-Publication Data

Rempel, Mark A.
    Point blank / Mark Rempel.
        p. cm.—(Extreme fiction series ; bk. 1)
    Summary: A senior class assignment prompts students to
consider past events that have shaped their philosophies of
life, leading two troubled boys to plan what will be the worst
school shooting in American history.
    ISBN 0-7852-6546-5 (pbk. : alk. paper)
    1. School shootings—Fiction. 2. Christian life—Fiction. 3.
High schools—Fiction. 4. Schools—Fiction. 5. Phoenix
(Ariz.)—Fiction. I. Title
    PZ7.R2838 Po 2002
    [Fic]—dc21   2002003473

Printed in the United States of America

02 03 04 05 06 QWB 5 4 3 2

To the families and students
of Columbine High School.

Your triumph is changing the world.

CHAPTER 1

"911 EMERGENCY."

"I heard shots everywhere," the caller screamed. The static coming from the connection was almost unbearable.

"Come back?"

"Shots—they're shooting again!"

"Where are you calling from?"

"What? What?"

"Where are you calling from?"

"School. The school. I'm in school."

"What school?"

Silence.

"Are you injured?"

Whimpering. All that could be heard was whimpering.

"Can I have your name?"

"Oh No! They're starting again! Help us! Send someone! I think they're coming this way. They're coming this way!"

"Who? Are you there? Stay on the line. You are calling from a cell phone. I need to know where you are so I can have a police car dispatched to your location immediately."

"Please send someone. I'm scared. I can hear their footsteps."

"Whose footsteps? Please settle down."

"They just shot one of my teachers. My teacher."

"What teacher? Who? Who's shooting?"

"History . . . my history teacher."

"Who shot your history teacher?" Silence. "Hello?"

"Two. I saw two of them."

"Two?"

"Yeah. I think."

"What school are you in?"

"School? It's Lincoln. Lincoln High."

"Where are you located in the school?"

"Janitor's closet. I don't know. I think I'm in the janitor's closet. Somewhere upstairs. I don't know." Phone static. "I don't know."

"Come back?"

No response, just static.

"I have to whisper. Oh, no, I think I hear someone coming."

The connection was getting worse.

"Are you there? Hello? Hello? Is anyone there?"

Heavy breathing. Silence. Boots walking. Glass crunching.

"Hello? Are you injured?"

"Shhh."

Silence again.

"I think he's gone."

"Are you injured?"

"I'm bleeding. My left arm is bleeding from the glass. Can you get my mom on the phone? I just want my mom. I just want my mom. I want to talk to my mom!"

Heavy breathing. Overwhelming sobs.

"Can you see anything going on in the building?"

"What? I can't see anything. It's dark in this closet."

"Can you tell me if anybody else in the building has been injured?"

"What? I told you, I don't know. I was in class and . . ."

Silence.

"And what?"

"I think they're coming back."

"Who's they?"

"They are. Please, God. No!"

"What is your name?"

"My name?"

A door handle turned. The heavy door protecting Lincoln's second-floor mop and broom closet opened slowly with a squeak.

"OH NO! NO! PLEASE, NO!"

The low dial tone sent the message that the phone connection had been cut off.

"Hello? Hello? Is anyone there? Please tell me someone is there."

The second-floor janitor's closet was now empty. A trail of blood was all that had been left behind.

CHAPTER 2

"Is THIS THING ON? Still dark. This is crazy. What button am I not pushing? Oh, I guess it helps if you take the lens cap off. Good one, Seth. You're bright. So bright your SAT scores will get you into the special education college of your choice. Enjoy the short bus . . ."

Seth checked one more time, by waving his hand in front of the lens, to make sure the camera was working before he stood in front of it.

"I think we're in business. Uh, this is Seth Anderson. Senior at Lincoln High School. I'm 5'9", well built, dark hair, brown eyes, and presently lookin' for a lady. No, this is stupid. Cut! I'll start over."

Seth cleared his throat and started over.

"Seth Anderson. Senior at Lincoln High School. Senior philosophy class. My senior project is to make a video that answers the question 'What is the meaning of life?' I'm no movie director, but it was either this or a ten-thousand-word essay on the subject. And, well, Mr. Danielson, you know how I am with words. I'm not sure how good this will be because I obviously had some issues with the lens cap."

The camera clicked off.

"Oh great. Now what?"

CHAPTER 3

"LIZ, TIME TO GET UP."

There was no movement. Bernice Clarabough tapped on her daughter's door again. "Did you hear me, Liz?"

Liz let out a big moan. Her mother opened the door wider now, only to find Liz's short 5'4" frame sprawled out on the floor beside her bed.

"Liz, what happened?"

"What?"

"How on earth did you get from your bed to the floor?"

Liz opened her eyes, focusing, on her surroundings. A sock, previously left on the bed, was stuck in her bright red hair. Liz pulled it out, staring at it oddly. "No idea, Mom. No idea."

Bernice started picking up the dirty laundry spread out on the floor. "You know, Liz, how many times have I told you, if you'd put your clothes away when you were done with them there wouldn't be such a big mess always left where you dropped them."

No comment. Liz only moaned again.

"I mean, how many times have you worn some of these? Once?"

Liz sat up. "Mom, I can take care of my own room.

Coming in here at 6:30 to tell me to pick up my room isn't a great way to start my day, all right?"

"Well, my dear, coming in here at 6:30 to see such a mess isn't a great way to start my day either. You're going to have to marry a neat freak or you'll both drown under all the laundry."

"I'll take care of it, Mother," Liz said sharply while standing and stretching.

"Well, I hope so. I'll take a load downstairs. Breakfast is ready."

"Give me a few seconds, all right? I just woke up."

Bernice took a load of dirty clothes in her arms and headed down the stairs of their upper-middle-class Arizona home. The family had just moved out to Chandler, a southern suburb of Phoenix, a year earlier. Although the children had thought it was for a job transfer, Bernice and her husband, Mark, knew that the reason went far deeper. It had been a last-ditch effort to save their only daughter's life. The crowd she had been hanging out with at her private school in Denver wasn't a positive one. Her daughter's involvement with witchcraft had left them torn and confused as a family.

"Thank You, Lord," Bernice whispered as she shoved the load of Liz's clothes into the washer. There wasn't a day that had gone by since Liz's life had been changed that she didn't thank God for the new life their daughter had been given.

Shortly before they moved, Liz had planned to run away. But after visiting Bernice's sister in Phoenix she changed her mind. A weekend retreat with her aunt's youth group caused Liz to make a 180-degree change in her life. One of the leaders who prayed with her at an altar that weekend said she couldn't get Liz to stop crying. Somehow, some way, God had broken through her metal heart. She came back to Denver changed.

"Liz, breakfast!"

"Coming."

When Bernice and Mark saw Liz slipping back into the peer pressure of the students at her school, they knew that a permanent change was needed. Although it hurt for Liz to leave, she wasn't opposed. Besides, she liked the hot weather and the fact that she could swim just about any day of the year.

Liz finished applying her eyeliner and closed her compact, putting it in her blue Gap backpack. She grabbed it by the strap and headed down the stairs to the kitchen. Since the move, Liz had made a conscious effort to really work on what she called her "relationship with God." Day after day, night after night, Liz would lock herself in her room singing and praising God. Embarrassed by her voice, Liz would sing softly so nobody could hear her singing. Also, it wasn't abnormal to find her asleep next to her Bible, sprawled out on the family room floor in the morning. For Bernice, it had been a miracle. For Liz, she had found the truth, and that truth had set her free. Free from all the crap that she once looked to give her life meaning.

"Where's Dad?"

Bernice poured herself a cup of coffee. "He had to fly back to Denver today, on business. He should be back by dinner tonight."

"Quick trip. I was hoping to talk to him this morning." Liz set a bowl of cereal on the island that was centered in the middle of their kitchen. Bernice had told her a hundred times not to do that.

"You were? Is there anything you can talk to me about?"

"Not anything you won't hype out about."

"Hype out, huh? Am I that bad?"

"Just on the weekends," Liz said back with a smile.

"Is it about that boy?"

"Boys? Mom, I can't talk to you about boys. You flip."

Bernice sat down at the table. "I'm all ears this morning. No flips. I promise."

"Cross your heart?"

Bernice made a cross with her fingers over the top of her chest. "Crossed."

Liz sat down now with two slices of toast loaded with peanut butter. "Well, that guy that likes me, uh, Seth, you know, Seth?"

"Go easy on the peanut butter, Liz. Yes, I know Seth."

"Well, he asked me to go with him to the prom. And, well, I'd like to say yes."

Bernice took a deep breath. She was ready to flip. Liz and her had such a special friendship. This entire situation with Seth seemed to be stretching their relationship in all kinds of new ways. Bernice sighed.

"There you go already, your pre-flipping exercise," Liz said with a mouthful of bread. The statement was almost incomprehensible because along with a mouthful of bread, Liz also had a mouthful of peanut butter.

"What?"

"You're breathing hard. I know you're gonna flip when you breathe hard."

Bernice took a sip of her coffee, trying to relax. "It's just that you know how your father and I feel about you dating someone who is not a Christian. Sweetheart, there are a million things that you and I agree on. But this is just one area that we don't."

"I know. That's why I wanted to talk to Dad. To explain a few things."

"Well," said her mother, taking a deep breath, "give me a try." She exhaled and tried to look calm. Her frown had been replaced with a plastic smile.

Liz was quiet for a moment, and then she spoke.

"First of all, he's a really nice guy. I mean, really nice. He's not like all the other jerks at Lincoln. He's into building a relationship, not trying to get something from me on the weekends. He opens the doors and carries my books. He's the first guy I've ever met who is like that."

"Now, Liz, how about the guys in youth group? Surely there is a gentleman there."

"You know, you'd think that. Some of them are

worse than the guys at school. They go to youth group to get one thing—"

"Liz!" Bernice responded, banging the heavy bottom of her coffee cup on the table.

"Well, it's true. You tell me why some of my friends at church are having sex as much as those who aren't in the church?"

"Where did you hear that?" Bernice tried to reply gently, taking another sip.

"Pastor Trevor. He says he can't figure it out either. Why would kids that have the answer choose to drown out the question?" Liz took her last bite of toast.

"Well, I can't speak for all of them, but I know there has got to be a young, Christian guy out there somewhere who doesn't want to have sex before marriage. I found your father, you know."

Liz rolled her eyes. "Oh great, here we go. Another episode of 'The Good Ol' Days.'"

"Make fun of me all you want. But back during the 'free love' movement, everyone was 'making love' and I felt like a dinosaur. My best friends laughed at me and said I would never find a virgin to marry. But when your father walked into my parents' diner, I knew he was different. But I had to wait. Every Friday my girlfriends would drive into downtown Denver and shack up with anybody that was cool enough to 'love.' Do you think I don't understand?"

"Different time, different place."

"Sweetheart, you're not listening."

Liz stood up and filled a glass with juice from the refrigerator. "Sure I am. Now, let's get back to the question of Seth taking me to the prom. Mom, I know he's not a Christian. But he's searching. I can feel it. We have talked for hours about my relationship with Christ. He's asked a million questions. And this philosophy project we're doing has caused him to think even more. Which reminds me, is the printer working? I have to print out my final copy today."

"I hope so."

"I'm late. We gotta go. So, what do you think, can I go?"

"You want an answer, here, right now?" Bernice glanced at the clock above the stove. Liz was going to be late.

"Sure, that'd be great," Liz replied, finishing off her juice.

"I don't think so, dear. We don't even know this boy."

"I'll bring him over."

"I'd love to meet him. But prom? We're already having a hard time just allowing you to go."

"But it's my senior year, Mom."

"I know," Bernice replied, looking into Liz's eyes. "We have already fought this battle. You can go. I trust you. I trust you not to drink, take drugs, go back to some of the things you left behind."

"Mom, don't you get it?" said Liz, raising her voice. "I'm not going to do those things. I let them go a long time ago. I hate what they did to me. You know that. Jesus is my life. He is everything to me. I can't get enough of Him. Trust me, all right?"

"It's just, ah, it's just so hard." Bernice wanted to give in. She felt a wall being built between her and Liz this morning. "After we saw how that stuff had ahold of you, to see you totally free is something we never want to lose."

"Then trust me. How can I ever be truly free if you don't ever let me out of your grip? 'Whom the Son sets free is free indeed.' Right?"

"I know. But there are some things you're going to just have to trust me on."

"I don't get this one. Why don't you trust my judgment about Seth? He isn't going to hurt me. He's the kind of guy that I want to date. Maybe he'll even accept Christ because of our relationship!"

"And what if he doesn't? What if you lose out on this one?"

"YOU JUST DON'T UNDERSTAND!" Liz yelled at the top of her voice, heading up the stairs to grab her journal from the bed stand.

Bernice set down her empty coffee cup. She was starting to feel the caffeine kick in and broke into a cold sweat. She didn't want the morning to end this way. She took the car keys out of her purse and set them on the table.

Liz ran down the stairs and through the kitchen.

"Where are you going? Aren't I driving you to school?"

"I'm taking the bus," she replied, stuffing an orange into her backpack.

"But what about the report?"

"I'll hand it in on Friday. Mr. Danielson likes me."
The door shut behind her with a slam.

Bernice stood and watched her daughter run down
the street to where a group of kids were standing.
She set her coffee cup in the sink with a sigh. "Why
did this morning have to end this way?" she whispered. Her thoughts wandered to picking Liz up
from school. Shopping—they would go shopping.
That always seemed to help when they weren't getting along. Liz had put a prom dress on hold until she
could save enough money to buy it. Bernice decided
that she would pick it up, pay the balance, and then
they could shop for shoes before Mark returned that
evening.

"That will make things better," she concluded. And
that's all she wanted, for things to be better.

CHAPTER 4

THE NEWS 4 VAN headed into the parking lot against
a tide of traffic. It traveled through the cars like a fish
swimming upstream. Several police cars had just
arrived with their lights flashing. Two policemen
were trying to set up barricades to keep anybody
from getting close to the school building. The white
van parked in a vacant handicap spot close to the
entrance. Out jumped a man from the driver's side
wearing sunglasses, jeans, and a faded Grateful Dead
T-shirt. From the passenger side stepped a tall, slender brunette wearing white pants, a short-sleeved
blue blouse, and a red ribbon that tied her hair back.
The ribbon was a makeshift, an afterthought. She
was in a rush. Her eyes glared down at the clipboard
in her hand. The man grabbed a camera from inside
the back door and rushed with the woman onto the
grass that led to the front entrance. If a story was
going to happen it would have to be right now,
before more cops came and the barricade was fully
functioning. But for now, all hell seemed to be breaking loose. Students were flooding out of the building, screaming at the top of their lungs as they ran
away from the school entrance doors. Yes, this was

the perfect time for a story. The closer to the building they could get, the better.

The woman stepped away from the pandemonium, standing, trying to keep her composure. She tried to wipe the fear from her face. The man with sunglasses handed her a microphone. He set the camera on his shoulder, pointing it in her direction. The red light on top of it began to flash. Ready or not, the reporting had to start now.

"This is Maria Severson reporting live from Channel 4 News with a late-breaking story. It has just been confirmed that several gunmen have started shooting inside Lincoln High School located at Ray and Arizona in the East Valley city of Chandler. No word has yet been given on how many students have been shot, or if the gunmen are still shooting, but the horrific scene here indicates that a tragedy has once again happened on one of our campuses."

A girl with blood streaming down her face ran behind Maria, screaming and crying. Again, she tried to remove any fear from her face. She had just finished a quick lunch after reporting about a local bank robbery a few streets away from Lincoln High. They had gotten a call from the station regarding a possible shooting at Lincoln that had been all over the police scanner. Since she was just a few streets away, Maria had been chosen to check on this exclusive report. What sounded like a great break for her wasn't feeling so great anymore.

"The scene here is overwhelming. Students and parents are running everywhere. The police and SWAT team have just arrived. The shooting began approximately ten minutes ago, when a 911 dispatcher got a call from a teenage girl stuck in a janitor's closet. Her whereabouts are unknown at this moment." Maria took a deep breath and stared at her clipboard for a few seconds. "Again, the gunmen's identities have not been established. All we know at this time is that shots have been fired and that some students have been hit."

"Maria," a voice echoed through her earphones from the Channel 4 news station, "have you heard any eyewitness accounts of what is happening inside the school?" Television viewers from around Phoenix were starting to tune in.

Maria shook her head. "No, Janet, I haven't."

A chill ran up Janet Theisen's spine. She crumpled the papers she was holding and wildly clicked the pen cap that was clenched between her right thumb and index finger. She blurted out another question. "Maria, is there a list of students that are still inside the school posted anywhere?"

"No, Jan, but it appears most of the students haven't exited the school. Only several hundred seem to be outside here on the grounds."

Janet sighed loudly. Her insides told her to make the most unprofessional move of her life by asking Maria if she could see her son out in front of the school anywhere, but she could get fired for doing something like that. Her thumb kept clicking the top of the pen.

The cameraman motioned to Maria to walk over to a group of students huddled together close to where their van was parked. Nervously, Maria headed in their direction. A cop ran by, screaming at them.

"Move, get away from the building. Move away!"

Janet scanned the students, looking for her son's familiar black concert T-shirt and ripped jeans.

"Excuse me, did you just exit the school?" Maria questioned the cluster of three students huddled in a circle. The question was barely out of her mouth when Maria realized that she was going to have to do better than this. She was going to be on national television.

Silence. Sobbing.

"Are you all right?" A few students ran behind Maria into the parking lot, screaming.

The camera focused in on the small group. The silence on the video screen in the newsroom made Janet nervous.

Maria spoke again. "Can you tell me what is going on inside?"

A young man with long blond hair and a nose ring looked up at her from the group she was now standing beside. "It was awful."

"What was awful?"

A young brunette tried to talk between heavy sobs. "He just started shooting at me. We were in philosophy class, and one minute we were watching this video thing and the next thing I heard this loud pop"—she started crying again—"and then my best friend fell to the ground!"

Janet squinted at the monitor to focus in on the girl's face. She looked familiar.

Maria kept prying. "Was your friend shot?"

"I don't know. She just fell right in front of me. I got on the floor and put my hands over my head. I didn't want to look. I didn't want to look!"

"How did you get out? How many students are still inside? Do you know how many students are inside?"

The girl started sobbing again, falling into the arms of the blond-haired boy. "Can you get your stupid camera out of our face! Don't you get it?" The group moved into the parking lot away from the scene.

Maria stepped back. Janet's eyes opened wide. The cameraman moved the shot from the students to Maria's face.

Janet broke the silence. "Thank you, Maria. That was Maria—"

Before the red camera light stopped blinking it recorded five shots fired through an upstairs window. At the sound of gunfire and breaking glass, Maria and the cameraman instinctively hit the ground. The cameraman felt like a combat photographer. Maria felt undignified. Janet watched the image spill to ground, focusing on a piece of the cement.

"Maria? Maria!" Janet screamed in a panic. She grabbed onto the newsroom counter to settle herself down and looked into the camera. "That was Maria

Severson reporting to you live from Lincoln High School, where an unknown number of gunmen are still inside the school." Her nails dug into the Formica with more force. "If you have a student who attends Lincoln, please do not panic. Again, do not panic or make assumptions." She broke into a cold sweat. "We will have all the late-breaking news as it develops. Now, back to you, John."

CHAPTER 5

"911 EMERGENCY."

Silence.

"Is anyone there? Can you talk? Hello?"

Margaret Owens, 911 day emergency dispatcher for the city of Chandler, tapped a pencil on the desk she was sitting at. This was the fifty-third call that she and a few other coworkers had received in the past five minutes. She had never experienced anything like this. Most emergencies had fixable endings. You sent a squad car or an ambulance, or dispatched a fire truck to take care of the problem. This time, though, something was different. Too many calls were coming from inside the school, where students were still hiding or trapped. Margaret couldn't fit all the pieces of the puzzle together. She knew there were shots coming from inside the school, but nobody knew who was shooting or why. The phone at the desk across from her rang. A fellow dispatcher answered. It, too, was from inside the school. Sweat drops ran down the back of her neck. She glanced at her computer screen; the call she had just answered was coming from inside the school again.

"Hang in there, we have officers on the way. Can you tell me your name?" Margaret could hear heavy breathing and whimpering.

"It's me."

Margaret glanced at the time; 11:52 A.M. *Me*, she thought, *who could "me" be?* After all, she had fielded a large number of calls in a handful of minutes.

"From the closet."

Immediately, it all made sense.

"Yes," she replied softly, "where are you now?"

"Uh, I don't know. Wait. Boys' bathroom. Second floor."

"Are you safe?"

"I think. I don't know."

"What happened?"

Silence.

"Are you still there?" Margaret said a number of times. It was her job to always keep the caller on the line.

"Yes. I was in the janitor's closet." Static again. "A guy from my philosophy class found me. He's been shot in the leg. He's bleeding everywhere. Oh God, he's bleeding everywhere. What do we do?"

"Try to settle down. Where is he now?"

"In the stall next to me. We have our feet up so if anyone comes in they won't see us. But the blood, it's dripping everywhere. It's all over the floor!" She started to cry again.

"You're going to be all right," Margaret reassured her. "All right? I mean it. You have my word. Now, is there anything, like a cloth or something, that you can put over the wound? I want you to try to put something on the wound and apply pressure. Gently, now."

"Uh, uh, I don't know." The girl looked down at her

feet. "My socks. One of my cheerleading socks. Would that work?"

"Uh, sure. Just something." Margaret had never advised dressing a wound with a sock, but if there was nothing else it would have to work. She listened closely as the girl struggled to get her sock off, and then moved into the stall where the young man was.

"Now what?"

"Do you see where the blood is coming from?"

"No, I mean, yes. Oh God, it's so gross. I can't do this."

"Yes you can. You can."

The girl started to sob again.

"Can you raise his leg? Use your sock and apply direct pressure to the wound." Margaret stopped. She heard a tremendous popping noise behind the heavy breathing. "Are you there?"

"Yeah. What was that?"

"Did it sound like the gunshots you heard before?"

"No. It was just one big bang. Oh God, what was it? What is it?"

Margaret signaled her supervisor over. She grabbed a piece of paper and scribbled a note.

I think there are bombs inside. Second floor. Close to the boys' rest room.

Her supervisor immediately radioed one of the squad cars in Lincoln High's parking lot.

Margaret heard another explosion. Then another. A scream from the girl on the other end of the line made the hair on the back of her neck stick up. Another explosion ripped through the phone line, almost causing Margaret to yank the earpiece out of her ear. It sounded like the bomb could have been planted somewhere in the bathroom.

The phone clicked off and a resonant dead tone told her ears that she wasn't helping any longer. Did she just hear the fate of two young lives?

Margaret grabbed her stomach. Her job wasn't just about emergencies now, but getting as many students out of that school as possible. Margaret clicked off. All she could do now was wait. She wanted to bring a message of hope. But that could only be done in person. For now, she would have to wait. The phone was the closest she was going to get.

"If there's a God in heaven," she whispered to herself, "I pray that You're with that girl. That You're with all of them."

CHAPTER 6

SETH TURNED THE VIDEO CAMERA'S POWER to the on position while walking up Cooper Severs's front steps. He didn't want to miss a beat. The project was due in less than two weeks, and that wasn't much time to get all the interviews he needed plus edit down the entire project. Driving, upbeat music could be heard bouncing through the front door. Laughter, screaming, and dancing; Seth could hear people dancing. His forehead started to sweat. He hated dancing. Partly because he didn't have any rhythm and partly because he knew that some girl he didn't know would probably ask him to dance. Most guys were afraid something like that wouldn't happen. Not Seth, he avoided it as much as possible. He sighed. Maybe after a few beers he'd feel comfortable. He knocked on the door. No response. Seth knocked again. Still nothing. He decided it was safe just to go in.

The scene was no different from any other weekend party he had been to during the last two years. The house was mostly filled with faces he knew and some he didn't. The lights were off, except for a few lamps and a strobe light somebody had plugged into the corner. A keg was on the kitchen table and under it a puddle was forming. All the cups were gone, so people were recycling them. The smell of alcohol burned Seth's nose.

"Hey, Seth." No response. Seth couldn't hear anybody above the music. "SETH!"

"Oh," he responded, "sorry. I can't hear a thing!"

"Seth! Hi!"

Seth raised the camera and watched the faces pass by through the lens. They were screaming and yelling into it. There was obviously a good vibe going on here. Everyone seemed to be enjoying the night.

"Dude, what's with the camera?" Cooper hollered at him while filling another plastic tumbler with beer. His large body frame and Arizona Cardinals jersey gave away his passion for his favorite sport, football. His stocky shoulders and long legs indicated that this young man was still growing. Cooper had always talked about playing in the NFL. If his body size was any indication, he might really get his chance.

"Our wonderful senior project, Coop. I thought you'd have one in your hand."

"What?"

"A camera. How do you plan on passing the project?"

Cooper pointed to his head. "It's all right up here. My brother took the class four years ago. He's a freakin' genius. Journalism major at Cal State. I've got his ten-thousand word essay right here in my hot little hands."

Seth looked at him and smiled. "Coop, that's cheating."

"We're in the same family, right? What's the difference? He'd help me if he was here, right?"

"I guess," replied Seth, "but what if you get caught?"

"I'll take my chances," Cooper replied, grabbing a handful of ice cubes out of the freezer and placing them in his glass. "I like cold beer, you know? Ice cold."

Seth focused the camera lens on Cooper's face. "Smile, Coop, you're my first interview."

Cooper smiled into the lens and screamed, "Yeah, baby! This is the life."

"Let's see here. All right, Coop, I'm going to ask you a question and all you need to do is answer it. Got that?"

"Piece of cake," Coop replied, taking another swig of beer from the plastic glass.

"Let's do it." Seth pushed the record button. "I am here with Cooper Severs, philosophy major, just kidding, at Lincoln High School in Chandler, Arizona. Tell me, Cooper, in your own words, 'what is the meaning of life?'"

Cooper laughed into the camera. He was starting to feel really drunk now. "Life," he said, cracking up. "What do I think the meaning of life is? It's this."

Cooper grabbed the lens and panned the camera around the house. The open architecture made it easy to see into most of the rooms on the first floor. Hands clasped plastic tumblers half full of beer, cigarettes, and a few joints. A few students were dancing in the corner of the family room. Two high school sweethearts were making out on the patio. A tall, slender girl with a letter jacket was lying at the bottom of the stairs next to her vomit.

"Life," his friend continued, "is one big party. It's all about feelin' good. Getting that right moment and doing whatever you want with it!" Cooper grabbed a girl passing by and started to kiss her. She pushed him away. "Ah, come on, Angela, you know you want me!" Cooper laughed into the camera again. "Life. It's about doing whatever you want. Wherever you want. You party every day until you die, so that when you're in the grave you can smile, knowing you didn't waste a single moment. Right, John?"

Cooper grabbed another student, pulling him close to his shoulder. "Did you hear what I said, John? It's all about not wasting a single moment. Right?"

John looked at him, puzzled. He wasn't as drunk as Cooper was. "Whatever you say, Coop. It's your place. You bought the beer and whatever you want, I'm in with."

"You know what, John? You break my heart!" Cooper squeezed his arm around John's shoulder. John broke away and walked off.

"That's what life is."

Seth hit the record button, shutting the camera off. "Thanks, Cooper."

"Anytime, man. Want a beer?"

CHAPTER 7

BERNICE SHUT THE CAR DOOR, grabbing Liz's dress, which was wrapped loosely in a clear, plastic bag. It sparkled in the sunlight. Bernice smiled to herself as she thought about what Liz's reaction would be when she picked her up. While she headed into the house she found herself humming the chorus of a hymn they sang last Sunday at church. She started to sing the words while climbing the stairs and hanging the dress in Liz's closet.

"When peace like a river attendeth my way, when sorrows like sea-billows roll; whatever my lot . . ."

She turned on the television that was located in the armoire in Liz's bedroom. "Thou has taught me to say . . ."

The volume was blaring, almost causing Bernice to lose her train of thought on what she was singing. "We interrupt your already scheduled programming for a special News 4 report with News 4's premier news team, Janet Theisen and John Davis."

"It is well . . ."

"Good morning. This is Janet Theisen with a special report . . ."

"It is well . . ."

"On a shooting that has taken place at Lincoln High School in Chandler."

"With my—" Bernice stopped dead in her tracks. The singing ceased as she focused her attention on the television screen.

"It is believed that around 11:40 this morning a number of gunmen opened fire in one of the classrooms at Lincoln. Reporter Maria Severson has been there and was one of the first people on the scene. Maria, what is happening right now?"

The television flashed to a scene of disorder and frenzy. Over Maria's shoulder squad cars, fire trucks, ambulances, and an FBI van and helicopter could be seen. It resembled a movie set. Real, but unrealistic to think that it could happen in such a safe community.

"As you can see Janet, things are extremely crazy here. Although NEWS 4 was the first on the scene, everyone except federal and state officers has been barricaded across the street. Students are still exiting from inside the school and the chain of events is still not clear."

Janet cut in. "Maria, do you know if the gunmen have stopped shooting?"

"We don't know any of that information yet. The FBI has just sent a SWAT team in through the east entrance. There is a rumor that the shooting started in one of the classrooms and that the gunmen are still inside. Several explosions have gone off in the west parking lot, and a number of windows have been blown out or shot through."

Bernice fell to her knees. Liz was there. All she could think about was the dress that hung in her closet and the shoes that they were going to buy after school. "Oh my God. Mark, where are you?"

Mark Clarabough stepped outside the gate area at Denver's International Airport. His briefcase was tightly tucked against his left side as he made his way through the United Airlines terminal. After his lunch appointment was over he would turn right around and walk down this same terminal again. He sighed. Being away from his family was the worst part of his job. Although Denver used to be home for him, it didn't matter. Home was where he wanted to be and his home was now in Phoenix. Every time he flew into Denver for work he had to remind himself that they had made the decision for Liz. He would do anything for his daughter. She was his pride and joy. He was so grateful that she seemed to be back to herself again. Mark was grateful for his sister-in-law, for her church, and especially her youth pastor. That combination seemed to be what had made the difference in Liz's life. He kept walking, noticing a rather large group of people gathered around a television in one of the terminal areas. Mark wondered if the president was speaking.

"Oh my, not again," said a lady, stepping away from the huddle and rushing past him.

"What? What is it?" he said, trying to stop her.

"Another school shooting. This country is going to hell," she remarked, moving on.

Mark stopped and shook his head. *What is going on?* he thought to himself. He glanced at the television screen, then his watch. No time. He would have to pick up all the details when he returned to the terminal later in the afternoon. "What a shame," he said out loud, heading toward the baggage claim to pick up a suitcase full of products to show his client. "What a shame."

Janet tapped her pen on the counter, waiting for Maria's response. John was sitting next to her, and he could tell she was nervous.

"Janet," Maria replied, "we still have no information about which students are still in the school. A list of missing students hasn't surfaced, and there could be three to four hundred students still inside."

Janet sighed.

"Maria," John cut in, "do you see a lot of wounded students?"

"Yes. Although I personally haven't seen anybody who has been shot, several bombs went off in the cafeteria and they sent shrapnel everywhere. Many of these students have already been rushed to nearby hospitals. John and Janet, the police are asking that no more parents come down to the school grounds at this point."

"What?" Bernice said back to the television. "They can't do that!"

"Why is that?" Janet asked Maria.

"Well, it's just pandemonium here. Until they stop the gunmen, nobody can go inside or even be in close proximity to the school grounds, even though the FBI and police have staked them out. They are busing all students to Borsche Elementary School, located at 456 South Beaver Canyon Road, to be picked up. If you cannot find your child there, then you should check the local hospitals and then the Red Cross, who are working closely with the police. They are stationed at the elementary school and the three local hospitals that victims have been sent to."

Bernice picked up the cordless phone from her dresser and frantically dialed her friend Mary Lou. "Hello, Mary Lou. Have you heard? Oh my God, my baby is there. I know, but how can I not panic? Liz could still be in that school. Yes, I know. Now? I'll be there in a second." Bernice hung up the phone so hard cracked a piece of plastic off the base. It fell to the floor. She grabbed her car keys, heading down the stairs and out the door.

"Mark," she mumbled. She had forgotten to call Mark on his cell. He would have to wait. She needed to pick up Mary Lou and get over to the school. They weren't going to keep her away. She wanted to find her baby. Bernice climbed into the car, backing out of the driveway with a squeal. "My baby, I know she's all right. I just know it. Dear God, help me to know it. Be with her, right now. Comfort her. Please, comfort her."

CHAPTER 8

DUANNE WEBB, the Maricopa County coroner, slammed his car door. He had parked across from the school. The grounds of Lincoln High looked mad.

"It looks like every squad car in the East Valley is here," he said to himself, "a good time to speed."

Duanne showed his county coroner badge to a cop standing outside the barricade. The policeman let him through, pointing him to the lieutenant who had been heading the operation since his arrival on the scene early that afternoon.

"Dr. Webb?"

"That's me."

Lieutenant Bill Nielson looked at his clipboard and checked off Webb's name. "It's a mess in there. Bomb disposal has been busy; they say it's all clear now, though. None of the bodies have been touched. They're all still where they were at the time of the shooting. Let me go over their locations with you."

"Lieutenant, how many are there?" Duanne said, cutting off Bill's comments.

Bill was silent. "We believe a total of sixteen are dead. Thirty are injured, depending on if they all survive at the hospitals. Five are still in critical condition."

"God help us."

The two men started heading toward the building. Books, backpacks, pens, pencils, and a shoe here and there littered the grounds leading up to the east entrance. Spots of blood colored the cement. The cellophane packaging from the paramedics' bandages lay on the grass like littered gum wrappers. Fragments of shattered glass were everywhere, a reminder of the powerful weapons the killers had used. Shell casings lined the sidewalk as the two men came to the door. It was a miracle there were no bodies lying lifeless outside the school walls.

"Dr. Webb, you are about to see the worst school shooting in history. You ready for this?"

"I see death every day, Lieutenant."

"No. I guarantee you, you've never seen this."

Nielson walked ahead of Duanne, leading him through the shattered doors of the east entrance. Duanne took a deep breath before entering. The smell of cordite was strong. "They shoot up this door?" he said to Nielson.

"This door and a bunch of others. They must have done it when they were running around the school."

Duanne's feet crunched on broken glass as he stepped inside the east hallway. It led to the school's creative arts auditorium.

"Look at those lockers," remarked the lieutenant.

A row of blue lockers was blown to pieces. Twisted metal littered the floor. Duanne stepped over a locker door.

"Some kind of explosive was planted in one of

these. Thank God it didn't go off at the right time. Hundreds of students were pouring down this hallway when the shooting began in a classroom on the west end. The classrooms on this side of the school were able to escape through this exit. Ten minutes later these bombs went off. Nobody was around then. Would have killed a bunch more."

The men continued down the hall. It reminded Duanne of a tornado that he had seen rip through the Midwestern town he had grown up in. There was stuff everywhere. Papers, locker doors, garbage cans, notebooks, backpacks, a trail of blood and glass; there was glass everywhere. Bullet holes covered the walls. One side of the hallway even had curse words spelled out from the fired ammunition.

It didn't take his mind long to figure out what the letters stood for. The hatred displayed that day was staggering. "Can you believe it?" he said out loud. He could hardly believe what he was seeing. "They even had time to spell out words with their gunfire. What a massacre. I've never seen anything like it." *Hope I never do again,* he thought to himself.

Duanne was starting to sweat under his white smock. This was harder than he had thought. Lieutenant Nielson led him into the auditorium.

"It looks like they made their way through the west wing, the cafeteria, the east wing, and then through here. By the time they got over to this side of the school a bulk of the students had time to escape. They went back to the west wing, and it looks like they killed themselves in one of the classrooms. We believe they had their guns and explosives in the backpacks they were wearing. They came in here and started shooting the curtains, the stage, and the seats. For some reason they tore apart the seats."

"Anyone in here?"

"A janitor."

Nielson quietly walked Dr. Webb to the mangled body. The bloody corpse was lying next to the stage.

"He never finished vacuuming," remarked the lieutenant, referring to the vacuum hose still in the janitor's hand.

Webb knelt down, examining the body closely. "Close range, in the back."

"Very close."

Dr. Webb took a pair of size 9 rubber gloves out of his smock and put them on. The snap startled Nielson. He had been a bit jittery since he had set foot on the campus.

Duanne put his finger into one of the bullet holes, sizing it out. "Large caliber?"

"Nine millimeter judging by the shell casings."

Duanne reached up, closing the janitor's eyes forever. "What a tragedy. This guy is probably in his late fifties."

"Fifty-seven. Frank McAllister. Employed by the school for twenty years. The teachers liked him and so did the kids. Why they killed him I don't know."

"I wonder if we ever will."

Webb stood up, taking off his gloves and throwing

them next to the body. "You can bag this one. I'll examine it at the morgue."

Nielson took a tag out of his pocket and tied it onto the janitor's finger.

"Where are most of the bodies?"

"Most of the shooting took place in a classroom down toward the west exit."

Webb and Nielson stepped away from the stage, heading out of the auditorium and into the hallway again.

"That body looked several hours old. What time did the shooting begin?"

"Noonish."

Duanne glanced at his watch: 5:03 P.M. He wondered if he had been doing this for too many years. "The killers. Where are they?"

"There is one self-inflicted in the classroom. But it looks like there might have been some kind of struggle. We know for sure that two were shooting. All of the pieces haven't come together yet. Eye-witnesses say that the two killers are dead in the classroom. You're the expert. I've seen a few suicides in my life. But these guys—these guys knew what they were doing. They definitely wanted to be dead when it was all over. Maybe one of them shot the other?"

"I'll take a look at where the bullets are lodged."

"Oh, and Dr. Webb, there is a lot of blood. Lots of it."

A man dressed in a flak jacket ran past them. Another one followed.

"Officer," hollered Nielson, "what's going on?"

The man stopped, turning Webb's way. "They think they found another explosive device in the library."

"What? I thought the building was clean."

"So did we. We just called the explosives team in again. I'm trying to evacuate the building."

"Continue."

Duanne shook his head. "Will it ever be over?"

"I suspect it's a false alarm. We had all the dogs and electronics that Phoenix could give. I think we got it all."

A blast shook the north part of the building. Nielson pushed Webb down onto the dirty floor.

"Get down!"

A second explosion occurred.

"Get out of the building, Duanne."

"What about you?"

"I've got men in that part of the building. I'll go."

"How safe is that?"

"Safe? There's nothing safe about Lincoln right now. Now get out of the building!"

Dr. Webb stood slowly and headed toward the east exit doors. His hopes of examining the dead quickly were gone now. He sighed. It was going to be a long night. Not to mention a long few days ahead.

CHAPTER 9

"ALL RIGHT, ALL RIGHT. Quiet down. I realize that you only have three weeks left of school. But that is still three weeks. That means we have a little more time together, seniors. So let's not ruin our relationship this close to the end. You have my word it will be an easy three weeks if you stick with me during it."

The second bell rang, signaling the official start of class. Mr. Danielson always liked to start his classes on time. That meant he got more time with the students. And that was why he loved to teach, for the students.

Every school has its heroes. Teachers that you know really want to be there. Teachers that go the extra mile, even when it inconveniences them personally. Nick Danielson was one of those. At thirty-five, he was still one of the youngest teachers on Lincoln's faculty lineup. He was a friend to all, even though many teachers resented his popularity with the students. He was charming, handsome, and he dressed like a teenager. It had been a rough year for him. Besides the heavy load Lincoln had him carrying, his daughter had come eight weeks early. He and his wife, Tracey, had spent many nights at Phoenix Children's Hospital during that time—so many nights that he knew the entire prenatal staff on a first-name basis. Now home, little Kasey was still receiving oxygen to breathe. But they hoped to have her off it by the end of the school year. Despite the struggle, many of the students in his classes had rallied around him. Especially fourth-hour philosophy. Filled with seniors, this class was his personal favorite. It was during this class period that he was able to analyze the meaning of life and give a generation struggling with questions a few answers.

The door creaked open. In walked Karissa Dalton. She smiled at everyone. "Oh, I'm late, aren't I?"

Mr. Danielson looked at the clock. "Well, at least you're consistent, Karissa. About three times a week you're a minimum of sixty seconds late."

Karissa laughed to herself and headed to her seat in the front row. The class laughed, too, and then stared. Liz wished somebody would measure her skirt, wondering if Lincoln even had some kind of dress code. Karissa always seemed to break the rules if there were any.

"Hey!" Crystal Lopez called out to Karissa from three seats behind her. "Did you get them?"

Karissa turned around and mouthed a "yes" with her lips. Crystal shrieked. Liz rolled her eyes. Karissa and Crystal were part of a group of girls at Lincoln known as Charlie's Angels. They were pretty, thin, and always dressed to kill. Liz told Bernice once that they were bigger flirts than Farrah Fawcett, Jaclyn Smith, or Kate Jackson had ever been. Karissa made most girls feel insecure with her presence, which made her friendship circle a small one.

"Today is the big day," Mr. Danielson continued. "Your semester projects are due."

The class moaned.

"I know, it's been a lot of work, but these projects are worth 50 percent of your grade. Our goal was to have you either write a ten-thousand word essay on what you think the meaning of life is, or to put together some kind of visual project where you interview everyone in this class about their thoughts and then end by sharing your own. So raise your hand if you decided to do the written project."

Hands went up all over the room. Nick looked back at his students, surprised.

"That seems strange. Okay, raise your hand if you decided to do the visual track for the project."

Two hands went up. Seth Anderson and Justin Le.

"Mr. Danielson," Justin blurted out.

"Yes," Nick said back.

"Uh, I did mine in Flash on the computer. CD-ROM. It's basically a Web page. You can click on all the information and interviews. Is that cool?"

The class moaned again. Only Justin would have put himself to work on a project of this magnitude. For him it meant that he could share his thoughts more artistically than on paper.

Nick Danielson thought for a moment and then replied, "I'll take a look at it, Justin, and then get back to you on it. Anybody else?"

Cooper raised his hand. "Uh, Mr. Danielson? I wrote eight songs about the project and put it on a CD for you. I've entitled my CD project, 'Butt Kisser'!"

Everyone laughed except Justin. He glared back at Cooper.

"Thank you for your contribution, Mr. Severs. I'll pop it in my stereo on the way home tonight. Now, let's move on. Seth, you have the only video project? All right, the rest of you bring your manuscripts and place them in the box next to my desk. Justin, you can set your CD-ROM in with the manuscripts."

Liz approached Mr. Danielson, who was erasing the board. "Mr. Danielson, can I talk to you for a moment?"

Nick looked at her, puzzled. "Uh, sure. Can this wait until after class?"

"No, it's about my assignment." A tear ran down her cheek. Nick knew it had to be now.

"All right, class, since you've all worked so hard on this assignment everyone can take five," he said to them. Then turning to Liz, "Let's step out into the hall-way, okay?"

She nodded her head, walking behind him to the door. Liz could smell Karissa's strong perfume as she walked by her on the way to the hallway. Karissa caught Liz's attention and mouthed the words "brown noser." Liz looked away. She and Karissa had never gotten along. Today was not the day for her just to ignore Karissa. She stopped for a moment. A warm tingle filled her neck and head. Liz made a fist with her right hand. All she wanted to do was turn around and hit her.

"Liz?" Mr. Danielson said to her, "are you coming?" He was waiting outside the door already.

"Uh, yeah" she replied, following him through the doorway. An echo broke the silence in the hallway as Nick shut the door.

"You all right, Liz?"

The tears started to roll again.

"Is it about the assignment?"

Liz shook her head. She could barely talk. "No," she finally muttered, "it's about my mom."

Mr. Danielson looked puzzled. "So, it's not about the assignment, but this is about your mom? I'm not getting it."

Liz controlled herself enough to speak. "I don't have it with me today."

"Well, we can figure something out. Can you bring it in after school? Or, is the bottom line that you don't have it completed?"

"No, no, Mr. Danielson, it's completed. That's not what I wanted to talk to you about. I don't care about the assignment. Even if I slip a grade or something, I'll get it in to you."

"Then what's wrong, Liz?"

"It's my mom. We got into an argument before I left for school. I don't know what to do about it."

Liz leaned up against the green wall. A few tears trickled onto the floor.

"What happened?"

"It's a long story. But, I really like Seth. And she doesn't. Well, it's not that she doesn't like him as a person; he's just not a Christian. He asked me to prom and I don't think they're going to let me go."

"With Seth?"

"Yes, with Seth."

"Tough call, huh?"

Liz nodded.

"Seth, he's a good kid. A really good kid." Nick paused for a moment before continuing. "But I know how much you really love your mom."

Liz nodded again, burying her head in her hands.

"Although Seth is an important person in your life right now, do you think this relationship with him is worth jeopardizing the one with your parents?"

Liz shook her head no. "But why do they make it so hard? He's so close."

"Close?"

"Close to knowing Christ. I know it. He's so close."

Mr. Danielson paused. "Then don't lose faith. But don't lose your parents either. Someone upstairs has got to be in control here, right?"

Liz nodded her head, wiping the tears away.

"Why don't you take a couple of minutes to get yourself together and," he said, taking some change from his pocket and placing it in the palm of her hand, "go give your mom a call. Let her know that you love her."

"Thanks, Mr. Danielson."

"Try to get your project in by tomorrow morning. Okay?"

"Okay," Liz replied. Her eyes felt itchy. She made her way to the girl's bathroom and rinsed her face and hands with cold water. After that she headed for the pay phone behind the cafeteria. She walked past a row of blue lockers and smelled the scent of gunpowder. Liz wrinkled her nose and stopped. She knew that smell well. Her father had hunted while living in Colorado. The smell of his guns after a trip had always filled the basement. A shrieking thought of violence ran through her head. She remembered watching an interview with a student who had been shot and yet escaped in a recent school shooting in Florida.

"That's crazy. Not at Lincoln," she whispered to herself and started to walk toward the cafeteria again.

Bernice parked the truck in the mall parking lot. The sun poured through the windshield.

"It's getting hot too early," she muttered to herself, shutting and locking the driver's door. As she walked away the cell phone that she had put in her glove compartment while driving started to ring. A delivery truck passed by her, muting the sound. Two rings, then three, four, and five.

"You've reached the cellular voice mail of Bernice Clarabough. Please leave a message after the beep."

A low tone resonated through the phone Liz was holding. "Uh, Mom, it's Liz. I just called to say that, well, I'm sorry about this morning and that I love you. I really love you. I don't want Seth to come between us. Okay? I hope you get this soon. I'll see you after school."

Click. Liz hung up the phone and headed back to class. Philosophy was officially half over now. She hurried through the hallway, not even thinking about the smell that had been there before. Although she hadn't gotten to talk to her mom, at least she had gotten through.

Bernice took the garment bag from the cashier and walked out of the dress shop that Liz had talked about so often. She headed through the maze of the mall in deep thought. What if Liz didn't know how much she loved her? Seth wasn't a bad guy, after all. Maybe she was being an overprotective mother. She hurried out to the car. Bernice wanted to hide the dress in Liz's closet. A better surprise than picking her up with it. This way they could shop for shoes and Liz could find the dress when she put them away in her closet. Bernice smiled. This was going to be good. She climbed inside the truck and started it up. This was turning out to be a much better day.

CHAPTER 10

SETH TURNED THE CAMERA ON, pointing it at Justin, who was now sitting at the computer lab desk. The project was due in two weeks. He had a lot of interviews to catch up on. His eye looked through the viewfinder. Darkness, again.

"Hey, try the lens cap," Thoran Le, or "Justin" as he liked to be called, said sarcastically.

"Oh, you're right," Seth said, taking off the lens cap. "I am interviewing Justin Le during fifth-hour computer lab. Justin, please answer the question, 'What is the meaning of life?'"

Justin squinted his eyes at the computer in front of him and kept working, ignoring Seth.

"Hello? Let's try this again. I am with the famous creative artist Justin Le, who is going to answer the question 'What is the meaning of life?'"

No reaction again from Justin. Seth started to get frustrated. "Come on, Justin. This is for my semester grade."

"So is this," his classmate shot back. "I've got my own project to do."

Seth kept pointing at him and saying, "Action."

Justin shook his head, finally breaking down. "All right. But only if you leave me alone after this. Deal?"

Seth shook the camera up and down.

Justin continued to focus on the screen. "Let's see, the meaning of life. Life, life." He paused and thought, then continued. "Life is all about what you can create and call your own. It's about how you express yourself as 'you.'" Justin looked into the camera lens. "For instance, take a look at this Web page I'm designing. Although it's ultimately not for me, there is a big part of me involved in it. I choose the graphics; I choose the colors. Life is made up of choices that I have to make. Those choices describe who I really am. Like the shoes I wear." Seth panned down to Justin's black Doc Martens. "These shoes describe a lot about who I am and what I like. Or, check out the shirt I'm wearing." Seth panned back up to the center of his shirt. "I made this design. It says, 'Justin Le Web Designs.' This describes even more about who I am."

Seth talked from behind the camera. "Cool. Now give us something deep. You always have something deep to say."

Justin shook his head. "Deep? This is deep. It's who I am. What more do you want?"

Justin focused his attention back to the computer screen. Deep? He didn't want anybody to go deep with him. *Deep is scary,* he thought to himself. Deep would mean seeing a few sides of Justin that he didn't want anybody to see. He wouldn't be able to hide behind his creativity. Creation for him was something he could easily hide behind. *No different than anybody else,* he continued thinking. Besides, deep would mean confessing to surfing all those pornographic sites that he seemed to find almost on a nightly basis. It was no big deal to admit to his friends that he was seeing them occasionally. In fact, it gave him something to help him fit in with his friends and to talk about. He just didn't want to tell them about the kind of sites he was surfing. That kind of honesty wasn't accepted at Lincoln, even though it seemed to be accepted by society. Maybe college would be different. The deep secret of his wanderings would have to stay buried in his heart, for now.

"One last chance, Justin. Come on," Seth hounded.

Justin turned his focus from the computer to the camera again. "Just be exactly who you are. That's it. If you're not that then you're just pretending to be someone else." Besides being a brilliant artist, he was also a great actor. "That's all I got, Seth. Turn it off, okay?"

"Somebody having a bad computer day?"

"Not me," replied a friendly voice from the other side of the table. Seth kept the camera recording. The lens focused in on Liz.

"I'm standing here with Elizabeth Clarabough. And to what do I owe this honor?"

Seth tried to wink at her with the one eye that was not behind the lens.

Liz smiled back. "Mr. Danielson. I'm working on my philosophy project."

"So am I."

"You took the easy way. I'm doing actual research."

"This is research!"

"What?"

"I'm researching you!"

Liz blushed. He was flirting and she loved every minute of it.

"So, Liz Clarabough, what do you think the meaning of life is?"

She paused for a moment. "It's simple. I think life is all about what you truly believe."

Seth smiled again. He loved to hear her point of view. It seemed so refreshing compared to everybody else's. There was something different about Liz. He couldn't put his finger on it.

"Because what you believe forms who you truly are."

Justin's voice could suddenly be heard in the background. "She's gonna get spiritual on us!"

"Justin! Quit. It's true."

Seth spoke to Liz, bringing it back to the interview. "So, what is it you believe in then?"

"I believe in living for a cause, because most people won't die for a dream or even a vision. But give them a cause to fight for, and they will be there."

Seth continued to egg her on. "And would that cause be something like 'save the whales'?"

"No. This is not about whales but about—" Liz paused. "Well, about Jesus Christ." She smiled into the camera.

The fire alarm belted through the hallways of

Lincoln. Its irritating buzz filtered into the second-floor computer lab. Several students stood up from their workstations, sauntering toward the door. No one seemed to be in a hurry.

Seth turned the camera on himself. "Gotta go!" he said, turning it off.

"This is the third drill this week. What's going on?"

"Probably some psycho with a bomb," Justin said snidely.

"That's not funny."

Seth put his camera in its bag and headed for the door. Liz followed close behind.

"Were you joking about what you said?"

"What?" said Liz, yelling back over the alarm.

"Was it real? What you said?"

Liz paused. "Very real. When you've been through what I've been through you can't hide behind what's fake."

They walked down the hallway with hundreds of other students, all pouring toward the east exit. Justin had decided to stay at the computer. He was having a creative moment.

Besides, he thought to himself, *who would ever think of bombing the school?*

CHAPTER 11

THE BLOUSE JANET THEISEN WAS WEARING was starting to soak through with sweat. The lights were warm and the subject heavy at News 4's downtown studio in Phoenix. Janet was nervous, very nervous. The shooting at Lincoln had become a news exclusive—and she was in charge. They were on the air every fifteen minutes with a local update for parents and the community at large. Nobody had mentioned the fact that Janet's son might be inside the school. Even Janet herself was afraid to say anything. After all, he was a senior, she had reasoned, and was responsible enough to get himself out of the situation. This was the biggest news story she had ever encountered. Leaving now would only jeopardize her career. CBS, NBC, and even CNN were on the phones hoping to get early, exclusive coverage that only News 4 had. This could be the breakthrough of her career. Or a nightmare for her as a mother. She couldn't believe how selfish she was being. But she now relied on the hope that her son was one of the screaming teenagers billowing out of the building with FBI agents standing all around them for safety. She scoured every piece of footage that came through to find her only son. As a single mother, she wanted a better life for her small family. A better life meant a bigger station or a national contract with a major network. Phoenix wasn't exactly a hub for talent scouts from New York or Los Angeles. This was the opportunity of a lifetime. *My only opportunity,* she thought to herself.

Her mind raced past all the hard work and time it had taken to get to where she was. It had only been three years since she and her son had moved out to Phoenix to start a new life. After interviewing for a receptionist's job at the News 4 station, her slender figure, beautiful skin, and charming personality became an asset to her in News 4's production office. It wasn't long before she was hired on as a field reporter for the station. She worked hard on every assignment she was given. So hard that she often found her son at home alone, waiting for his mother to come and tuck him into bed. A nasty divorce had left her only boy heartbroken and bitter. Janet had figured that the new life they had started in Phoenix would change everything. It had, just in ways she wasn't prepared for.

"Janet," the News 4 evening producer said to her in a frenzy, "you're up with the next quarterly hour report. We've had over two hundred calls from parents wanting information. This is big! Because we have the exclusive, more people are watching us than channels 10 or 3. NBC wants to use you and Maria in their special broadcast in the next hour. Can you stay a little longer and swing that?"

Janet smiled on the inside. "Could I swing it? What do you think? Of course I can swing it!"

"Good. You're on. They want aggressive reporting. Jane Pauley style. None of this Katie Couric stuff. Got it?"

"Aggressive. You know me, Tim."

"Good. It will keep the ratings up if they know we're going to be on a special NBC report. Janet, you've got to be good."

Janet primped her hair and sat back in her chair. This could be the greatest move of her career life. For a moment she thought of the school, the teenagers who had been shot, and her son—she thought a lot about her son. She felt guilty for building a career move on such a tragedy. But then again, business was business. "The world is all about power and money," she reassured herself. "I've got to do something for me. For us. Everything will be all right."

"Ms. Theisen, you're on in sixty . . ."

CHAPTER 12

MARK CLARABOUGH CLIMBED INTO THE TAXI that he had flagged down outside Denver's International Airport. He threw his briefcase and the small black suitcase into the backseat while climbing in.

"Downtown," he barked at the driver, "Bank One Building."

The taxi driver nodded and took off. Mark took his Franklin Planner out of his briefcase. He took a picture of himself and Liz out of the front inside pocket. They had taken it last winter, while skiing in Colorado. Mark had his right arm wrapped tightly around her shoulder. Liz was smiling. He loved to see her smile. It reminded him of how thankful he needed to be when he thought about all the days she used to wear a frown. His index finger ran across the cheek and chin of Liz's face. Something inside him wanted to be home. *This is just a day trip,* he had to remind himself. *Not even twenty-four hours,* he thought again. Liz loved chocolate chip cookies. He decided he would pick up a dozen of her favorites from a special bakery that they used to frequent in the east part of the city. It would take some cash to get a taxi down there and then to the airport, but Liz was worth it. He pulled out another picture of his older son, Ryan. He was away at his first year of college at Northern Arizona University in Flagstaff. It was a suitcase school. Almost every other weekend Ryan would make the three-hour drive home to see his parents in the East Valley. Mark missed him, too.

The driver accelerated his speed, turning onto an access ramp that led to I-25. They were heading for Denver's downtown area. Mark stared out the window, almost feeling as if he had never left the city. If he closed his eyes he could almost believe he and the family had never moved. But that would mean not seeing Liz's life changed. He opened his eyes again.

"Do you mind if I turn on the radio?" the driver said to Mark in a thick accent.

"No, that's all right with me. Go ahead."

The driver turned the knob next to the cassette deck. The news came blaring on . . .

"Once again, another school shooting has shocked the country. More coming up right after this message."

"Have you heard much about the shooting?" Mark asked.

"No, not much. Just that one happened again."

"You don't recall any details, do you?"

"No. Sorry."

"Just wondering."

Mark rolled down his window a bit to take in some of the fresh mountain air. The sun was shining brightly on the Rocky Mountains out the window to his left.

The commercial faded while the radio news music

increased in volume. "This is KWYZ's On the Hour News. Stay tuned for all the latest headlines. Here is your KWYZ news director, Tom Allen."

A rich, low voice took to the airwaves. "While most of us were working this morning, tragedy hit yet another school in our nation. Random shooting began in the late morning at Lincoln High School in the East Valley of Phoenix, Arizona."

Mark sighed. *Another school,* he thought to himself. *And in Arizona.* For a few seconds he almost forgot he lived there. The comfort of the Rocky Mountains and the skyline of Denver's downtown only reminded him of what home used to feel like. *Arizona?* he thought again.

"ARIZONA!" he said out loud.

"Excuse me?" the driver replied.

"That's where I live. Oh my God, that's my daughter's school! Lincoln is her school! Turn it up!"

He fumbled through his bag, grabbing his cell phone. His hand was shaking as he tried to dial Bernice's cell number.

"The cellular customer you wish to reach is not answering or is out of range. Push the pound key to leave a message."

Mark pushed it violently. A beep was heard. He spoke with fear.

"Bernice, it's Mark. I just heard. I am on my way back to the airport. I just heard on the radio. It's Liz's school. There was a shooting. I pray you're there already. Or maybe she stayed home. Call me as soon as you get this message." He signed off by pushing the end button. He squinted his eyes in the direction of the Rockies again.

"Turn around. I need you to turn around."

"What?"

"The airport. Get me back to the airport. If my daughter is in that school I'm not going to leave her there. I will get her out. I WILL!"

He pounded his knee with his fist. Mark grabbed his planner again out of his briefcase. He took out the picture of Liz. "Oh God, take care of her. She's my baby. My only daughter. Please rest Your hand on her."

The taxi turned off onto an exit and then back onto the interstate in the opposite direction it had been going. The sales call would have to wait. Missing a sale didn't matter much to him right now. His thoughts were on Liz.

"Hold on, Liz, hold on."

CHAPTER 13

BERNICE CLARABOUGH TURNED OFF THE NEWS she was listening to as she made her way through the upper class neighborhood in Chandler, Arizona.

What is the house number? she thought to herself. Bernice reached in her purse and pulled out a piece of scratch paper. Her mind was too jumbled to remember the number. She had written it down on the paper a few weeks earlier when she had picked up Mary Lou for lunch. "2334 . . . I think it's 2334," she whispered to herself. "Oh, there it is."

Bernice turned into a driveway that led to a large, beautiful stucco home. Mary Lou was waiting nervously on the front porch waving at Bernice.

"How are you doing, Bernice?" said Mary Lou, climbing into the 4 x 4.

"I don't know. My mind is like Jell-O. Have you heard anything new?"

"Well, I think I may have some good news. Ginger Talion called me and said her daughter had just called from a cell phone and reported seeing Denalyn outside Lincoln."

"Thank God for you. Did she see Liz?"

Mary Lou paused. She could feel the hope in

Bernice's voice. "Uh, no, she didn't say anything about Liz."

Bernice put the SUV in reverse. She jammed on the brakes, suddenly noticing she had almost backed into a truck in the driveway across the street. Her shaking hands grabbed the steering wheel, turning the vehicle away from a near accident. Bernice changed her perspective. She tried to find hope in something.

"Well, that doesn't mean she's not there. Let's go and check at Lincoln and then at Borsche. Denalyn and Liz are fine. I know it. They've got to be in that mess somewhere."

"I'm sure they are. Let's believe it."

"I've got to get ahold of myself, Mary Lou, or I'm going to crumble. My daughter is not lying dead in that school. She's not."

Bernice drove through the busy streets of Chandler. Traffic was heavy for it being shortly after noon in the Phoenix suburb.

"Oh my, look at that," Bernice shot out, stepping on the brake. "I think they closed Arizona."

Traffic along Arizona Avenue had come to a halt. A yellow plastic "Police Line: Do Not Cross" tape had been tied to the two stoplights that led into the main entrance of Lincoln High. Police cars lined the sidewalks and open areas around the north end of the campus.

"Bernice, turn here, down Third Street. There has got to be a way in."

Bernice cranked her wheel left as hard as she could, managing to turn down Third Street. They parked in front of a vacant house with the windows broken out of it. Traffic from the overloaded intersection streamed by at an overwhelmingly fast pace. Fear was in the air. Parents and friends of students rushed down the sidewalks, trying to get a glimpse of the school, and more important, a glimpse of someone they loved. Bernice started to cry.

"Mary Lou, I can't believe this is really happening. I thought we would drive down here and maybe find out that the whole thing wasn't true. Look at the people! The police. Something is very wrong here. I can feel it."

Mary Lou sighed, putting her arm around Bernice's shoulder. She tried to give her strength. She wanted both of them to "find their girls."

"Please stay with me today. Mark's in Denver, I need somebody. Just someone."

"We are in this together. I'm not going anywhere. I'm with you. Now let's go find them."

Bernice climbed out of the driver's side of the vehicle and waited for Mary Lou to join her on the sidewalk. They weren't alone. They joined a group of more than twenty parents walking toward Lincoln's main entrance. There wasn't much talking going on. The shock of the moment was starting to sink in. Bernice listened to a woman walking in front of her.

"I can't believe it. My sister told me that Lincoln was ranked one of the safest schools in the metro

Phoenix area. It seems almost impossible. How could kids get guns into the school? Didn't somebody see them? Didn't somebody know?"

Bernice was getting agitated. This woman was talking like a bystander, not a parent. Her detached indignance was a sharp contrast to the panic Bernice felt in her own heart.

Bernice's stomach started to hurt. Her palms were sweating along with her feet. More parents joined them. Businessmen. Construction workers. Women dressed in fine jewelry. Women not dressed beautifully at all. All kinds. All sorts. Right now, the place you lived or the amount of money you made didn't matter. The color of their skin seemed to be all the same. All that mattered was finding your child and running away from the school to safety.

Bernice and Mary Lou heard screams as they reached the intersection on Arizona Avenue that was set up as the main entrance to the school. A young girl ran into the woman's arms that had been walking in front of Bernice.

The young girl was crying and her mother tried to console her. "Oh baby, you're all right. Thank God! You're all right."

Other students were sprinting across the closed street, randomly yelling, even screaming for a face they recognized.

"Mom! Mom!"

"Thomas? Has anybody seen Thomas Morton?"

"Alicia? Alicia!"

"Dad, Dad! I'm over here!"

"I can't find her. I can't find her!"

Bernice fought her way through the crowd and cornered a policeman who was standing on the edge of Arizona. He was pushing parents back, keeping them from crossing the street onto Lincoln's campus.

"Officer, excuse me," she said loudly.

He ignored her.

"SIR! I need some information! SIR!"

"You're gonna have to back up, ma'am."

The scene over at the school evoked panic. The barricade kept parents from running to their children even if they did see them. The police were trying to get statements from some of the students who had escaped. Paramedics were treating minor injuries. Maps, papers, and blueprints were spread out on the hoods of squad cars like makeshift desks.

Bernice took a step back into Mary Lou; she spoke to the officer again. "Are there still students inside the school?"

The policeman grabbed a man trying to cross in front of them and pushed him back into the crowd. "Sir, no one is allowed to cross the street. No one!"

The man he pushed back into the crowd was angry. "Who do you think you are? Are you telling me I can't go in? My daughter is in there; is yours? Huh? Who knows how many mad gunmen are in there. Do you just expect us to stand out here knowing our own flesh and blood could be dying inside?"

The officer stood firmly in front of him now.

There was no way he was going to allow anybody through.

"Hey, Officer," the man called out, planting his fist into the policeman's cheek. Hysteria had now started. Mary Lou screamed. Her voice could be heard around the crowded area. Parents started pushing against the barricade. There was a definite sense that things on this side of the police line were also out of control.

The blow to the officer's face was so strong that it caused him to fall to the ground. Bernice knelt down beside him. Another policeman nearby came running over to deal with the problem.

"What have you done!" she cried out to the man who had just hit the downed officer.

"Nobody will hold me back from those monsters. Our kids are inside! Don't you realize that?" he yelled back, stepping onto the street. Several police officers ran through the crowd after the man, who was now sprinting toward the front doors. A nearby SWAT team also ran after him, circling in and bringing him to the ground. Little did the man know it was for his own safety.

Sirens could be heard in the distance. Bernice grabbed the officer's hand and squeezed it while directing Mary Lou to find a tissue for his bloody nose.

"You're going to be all right," she said softly into his ear. Several officers and two EMT's were now there.

"Did you see this?" an alarmed sergeant asked Bernice.

"Uh, yes, I did."

"What on earth happened here?"

Bernice tried to talk, but the shock was setting in. "I, I asked the officer for some information, and this man just hit him in the face and ran toward the school."

"What words were exchanged?"

Bernice wiped the sweat from her forehead. "Not much. The man wanted the officer to let him into the school to stop whatever is going on inside."

An ambulance arrived and broke up the crowd. The officer was transferred to a stretcher.

"I will need a full statement from you."

Bernice took a Kleenex from her purse and wiped the blood from her hand. A hand on her shoulder indicated to her that Mary Lou was still there.

"Mary Lou, what just happened?" she stammered. "Is any of this real? What is happening? I'm starting to feel really dizzy. I need to sit down." Before they could find a place to rest, Bernice fainted, falling on the sidewalk across from Lincoln High.

"Bernice?" Mary Lou yelled. "Bernice! Oh, somebody help me. Somebody help us!"

CHAPTER 14

"BUILDING IS CLEAN, SIR."

"Thank you, Officer," Lieutenant Nielson said with a nod. Bill spit the toothpick that he had been chewing onto the ground as he paced outside the east exit of the school. "Can you get an officer to go get Dr. Webb? Let him know we're ready now."

Duanne Webb stirred the sugar into his coffee and covered the Styrofoam cup with a plastic lid. He glanced at his watch, sighing. He had been waiting three hours for clearance to go back into the school. The press were waiting anxiously for answers, along with a crowd of parents who stood across the street from the now hushed educational institution. Duanne knew that the entire process had taken much longer than anyone had expected. Word had been given hours ago that the shooting had stopped and the bodies had been found. But until the school was clear of any kind of explosives, nobody could enter.

It was getting dark now. The police had set up flood-lights throughout the parking lot. They were bright enough to make your eyes squint. In many ways the investigation was just getting under way. Although the building was clear, the questions were just beginning. Duanne wanted to get in and out of the entire scene.

The pressure was starting to mount as he realized the ramifications this massacre would have on American history.

"C'mon," he said to himself, "hurry up."

He poked open the lid, taking a sip of the hot coffee. Duanne stepped outside the Circle K convenience store that was catercornered to Lincoln High. Once littered with students, it had now become the quick-energy snack shop for officers, agents, and reporters. The phone outside the store was in use again. Duanne wondered how many students had used it today. He remembered hearing several students talking to loved ones earlier, letting them know they were safe and sound.

"Excuse me, Dr. Webb?" a passing police officer said.

"That's me."

"Lieutenant Nielson sent me over to tell you that he got the all clear for you to head back into the school."

"Rock and roll. Let's go."

Both men walked over to the heavily guarded west exit where the shooting had possibly ended. Bill met Duanne there. They exchanged glances and stepped through the blown-out doors.

"Let's try this again," Duanne muttered, stepping over the cracked glass.

"Can I have your coffee?" an officer asked Duanne. "Crime scene."

"What?"

"Sorry."

"I won't spill it, promise," Duanne remarked, swigging down another sip.

"Thank you for your help, Officer," the lieutenant remarked, signaling with his eyes that the coffee was all right.

"I think she's all clear now, Doctor," Nielson said, "Sorry this has taken so long. But I don't really know what to think. This place was wired like one big booby trap. There was stuff everywhere."

"Did anyone get hurt in that last explosion?"

"No, not really. My men are just freaked. You hear about this all over the news, but when it happens you're never ready."

They passed by the auditorium again. Cordite was still in the air.

"Do we need to see the body again?" Bill asked.

"No. We tagged it. Let's get it out of here."

The two men turned down a long corridor that led to the lunchroom.

"From what I can tell," Bill continued, "they made their way down this hallway and into the lunchroom. Second lunch had just started. The next two bodies are over here."

Blood drops led to a long lunch table with two bodies underneath it. Duanne squatted down. A sandy-haired boy was lying facedown on the floor. His feet stuck out from under the table. His hand was still tightly clenching a brown lunch bag. Before Duanne examined the first body, he snapped on a pair of rubber gloves.

"Range doesn't look too close. Let me get an officer in here to mark where the bodies are. It appears that the shooters set up a cross fire. It looks like they were firing from both sides of the lunchroom. These kids must have tried to get away."

"Must have," Duanne commented, checking the body and recording the time on a clipboard. He closed the boy's eyes. "Is it me, or is it a miracle there aren't more kids dead in here? A cross fire should have hit ten or fifteen at the very least. It just seems odd to me."

"Somebody was watching over them."

Somebody? thought Duanne. The voices in his head wandered around the thought of a "God," but there were too many questions. Dealing with death on a daily basis, sometimes violent death, didn't always bring a ton of answers. *Why would a God allow this? Couldn't He have stopped this nightmare?* Duanne continued on in his thoughts. *Why?*

Tangled underneath a chair just a few feet away was a young girl wearing a cheerleading uniform.

"Looks to me like she suffered an early close-range wound to her arm, and these two bullets came later. Any theories?"

Bill paused for a moment. "Maybe she saw it coming. Or had been wounded earlier and was trying to tell someone."

"Maybe."

Duanne reached down. He closed her eyes, tagged both bodies, and stood up. "Man, I wish this was it."

"Oh, this is just the beginning."

Duanne snapped off his gloves and grabbed his coffee. Bill led him through the maze of books, tables, chairs, and trophy cases that had been shot to pieces.

"Let's head down to the classroom area."

Duanne could hardly keep the now lukewarm coffee down his throat. This entire situation was making him sick. It was one thing to see older bodies on a daily basis come through the morgue, but such young lives? How, and why? Duanne thought of his thirteen-year-old daughter, who lived in Vancouver with her mother. He couldn't stomach the thought of closing her eyes for good.

Duanne had seen a lot of violence in his day. But this—nothing could compare to what he was feeling at this moment.

CHAPTER 15

MARGARET OWENS HADN'T CHEWED her fingernails since she was in junior high. Her mother had insisted she wear that goop that tasted like rotten apples on her nails to get her to stop. As much as she had hated it at the time, the strange formula had worked. She hadn't chewed a nail since, until now. Today she felt like a scared little girl again. She stared impatiently at the blue computer screen in front of her. She was waiting, hoping for the phone to ring. Most days she dreaded the high-pitched sound that resonated from the speaker planted somewhere in the PC on her desk. Calls made her nervous. Lives were on the line, and she never wanted to make a mistake if a life could be saved. Saved. She wondered if the girl inside Lincoln High's-second-floor bathroom had been saved. Margaret fantasized about an FBI unit storming into the school and finding this young girl curled up on the floor. In her mind she would meet her a few days later. They would embrace and Margaret would really get to see the difference her life had made by helping someone to stay alive.

The calls from inside the school had tapered off. That was a good sign, her boss had said. That meant most of the students were probably out. The switchboard was still being barraged with calls from well-meaning citizens who didn't think the police department knew anything about what was happening inside the East Valley high school. Margaret's phone had been set aside to answer calls that were coming from inside the school. After her lunch break she had asked for the same assignment, in case her morning caller called back. It was getting close to 2:00 P.M., more than an hour since her last call. Margaret's hopes were quickly diminishing. She started to pray again and then wondered whom she was praying to. Was God really listening? If so, why was this even happening, here in her own hometown? Now the world would only remember Chandler as a place of tragedy, not tranquillity.

A ring shot through the computer system. The number was not traceable. A cell phone. It was a cell call again.

"That's got to be her. That's got to be her!" she said to herself. "I've got her! I've got her!" she exclaimed to the room.

The woman sitting next to her pulled her earphone off to hear the conversation.

"911. What's your emergency?"

There was a long pause, as before.

"Are you there? Is anyone there?" Margaret was starting to get emotional. Her voice started to rise as tears filled her eyes.

She heard a sniff, followed by a shaky voice. "I'm here."

Margaret smiled. "Thank God! I've been waiting for you to call!"

"I've been waiting to call!"

"What happened? Are you all right?"

"Yeah, so far."

"Where are you now?"

"Same place. I don't want to move."

"The explosion. Where was that?"

"I think it was the garbage can. They were throwing bombs outside the bathroom. The door opened and one came in here. I threw it in the trash can and we hid in the last stall. That's when I screamed. Sorry I dropped the phone."

"Sorry? No sorry needed here. You're very brave. Do you know what's going on in your area of the school?"

"Uh, Toby and I have just been hiding here for a while. After the bombs, we were afraid to leave. We thought maybe there would be another one in here. The stall was the safest place."

"How is your friend? Last time we talked he was bleeding pretty bad."

"I think he passed out. He's breathing. Just lying next to me."

Margaret tapped a pen on her screen. "Can you get his pulse for me? Grab his right arm and find an artery."

"Uh, I can't."

"Why?"

"His right arm isn't there."

Margaret's eyes opened wide. A drop of sweat fell from her head, oozing in between the keyboard keys. "Oh, no!"

"No, no. It's not what you think. He doesn't have a right arm. Never did. Ever since I've known him. Cancer or something."

The lady next to Margaret was standing now. Both women sighed. "Well," Margaret said, "that's good to know." Margaret paused. She felt awkward. "Not that his arm was gone, but that the explosion didn't do it."

"Nope. Nothing really hit us. The stall kept us safe."

"Thank God."

"You thanking God, too? Miracle stuff. It's all one big miracle."

"When is the last time you heard shots?"

"About an hour ago. We heard two. That was it. We heard somebody crying then. It was really weird."

"Did you see anything?"

"I wasn't going to go anywhere. I haven't heard a thing. Everything is quiet."

"Do you think the gunmen are still alive?" Margaret was doing everything she could to keep her talking.

"I don't know."

A crowd had developed around Margaret's desk. Dispatchers off-duty, dispatchers on-duty, even her boss was there, listening intently to every word said. This young girl had found a special place in their hearts. She represented what they wanted every student in that school to be . . . alive.

Margaret started to cry. Softly.

"Are you crying?"

"I'm sorry. Not very professional, am I? It's just that, I'm glad you're alive."

"So am I."

"Listen, can you reach over and check the pulse on your friend's left wrist?"

"Just a second."

The crew listening could hear shuffling, a door opening. The glass under the girl's feet was crunching loudly.

"I don't have a watch."

"That's okay. I'll tell you when to start. You just count heartbeats. Did you find the pulse?"

"Right here."

"Start . . ."

"1, 2, 3 . . ." The numbers trailed, forming a whisper.

Margaret watched her screen clock as it counted the seconds down. "Okay, stop. Whatcha got?"

"I think 50. Or 51."

Margaret knew that was low. Her stomach formed another knot.

"So he's alive, right?" the voice asked.

"Yes, he's alive. But if we don't get someone to him soon it may mean trouble."

Shock was starting to set in on Toby's body. Blood was still leaking from his leg wounds.

"Is there anything that you could lay over his body? A blanket?"

"I'm in a bathroom."

"I know, I know. Sorry."

"Would my cheerleading sweater be enough?"

"Yes, yes. Let's try it. Lay it over his shoulders and chest. We want to keep his body warm."

Margaret could hear her friend struggle to take off the sweater. She was overwhelmed even thinking about what this young teenager was going through. "You're doing great, you know. A regular nurse."

"Really? I'm just glad I wore my cheerleading outfit today."

"You're a walking first-aid kit."

Margaret heard a faint laugh. It was good to know that the girl was smiling.

"Listen, let's keep talking. As long as we can. Or until someone comes to rescue you."

"Someone already has."

Margaret paused. "Are you still in the school?"

"Yes."

"Who's there? The cops? FBI? What?" Margaret said, her heart leaping.

"Not a person. Somebody else has rescued me."

Margaret was puzzled now. She wondered if this girl was going into shock. "Who, sweetheart?"

"Jesus. My, ah, best friend. Just a minute, I'm getting light-headed. I'm going to sit down."

The crowd around Margaret's station had grown to more than twenty people.

"Really?" Margaret said with hesitation.

"Yes. If it weren't for Him, I wouldn't have made it through this. No way."

"So, how did He help you through?" she said, almost

patronizing her. Margaret wondered if this young girl was starting to hallucinate because of the trauma. "Did you see Him?"

"I wish. No appearances. Just His presence."

Margaret listened closer. Something felt genuine, almost real in what this young girl was saying.

"He is here. He's like this secret strength. When I was really scared an hour ago, I just started to pray. Immediately after I screamed I stopped crying. I could tell He was with me. It's weird, it's almost like His arms were around me."

Margaret felt a hand on her shoulder. She was weeping quietly now.

"Wow, that sounds like some kind of relationship."

"Oh, it is. I found Jesus, like, about a year ago. My mom died in a car accident in New Mexico. I was really mad at God. But my best friend, Liz, told me about how God had really helped her through a hard time. She moved here about the same time I did. So, we talked a lot. And I decided if God could help her, then He could do the same for me. Right there in fourth-hour philosophy I accepted Him into my heart. Can you believe it?"

The faces around the cubicle reflected Margaret's empathy now.

"It's weird," Margaret said back tenderly, "you called me for help. That's what 911 is for. And somehow, I'm receiving strength from you."

"Really? That's cool. That's God. He's real, you know. If He wasn't, I wouldn't be alive."

"I know."

"Listen, would you like to accept Him into your life?"

Margaret tried to compose herself. She used a Kleenex to wipe away the tears streaming down her face.

"Oh, I don't know."

"Sure you do. I just told you."

"I know. But you don't know me. I'm just a voice. There's a lot behind this phone. Things a young girl like you would never understand. Things I don't even know if I do . . ."

"Yeah, that's how I feel about my mom some- times . . . do . . . mean?" The girl's voice was starting to fade out.

"Are you there?"

"Yes, are . . . there?"

"Hello?"

"Battery . . . low. Wait . . . ," the voice responded back, crackling then cutting off.

"Hello? Hello? Are you there?"

The empty blue screen was reflected in Margaret's glasses.

"Oh, I can't believe this. We were so close," her boss responded angrily.

"Yes," responded Margaret with glassy eyes, "we were close."

CHAPTER 16

MR. DANIELSON CLOSED THE DOOR after talking to Liz out in the hallway. The class seemed out of control at this point. It was nothing too shocking for a class of seniors three weeks before graduation. "All right, everyone. Find your seats, please."

They continued to talk. Nothing was getting through. He put his fingers in his mouth and whistled as loudly as he could. The class immediately froze.

"It's a less dignified way to get attention, but it usually works. Now, will everyone find their seats, please."

The class quickly sat down.

"Say, Mr. Danielson," said John from the back, "what if you don't have your project today?"

"I wish you would have told me earlier. Is this something that you need an extension on, or that you don't plan on doing?"

John glared back. "It's done. I just have a few final touches that I want to add."

Nick noticed the large bag under his desk. "Are you sure you don't have a ten-thousand word essay in that pack somewhere?"

"I'm sure," John responded angrily.

"Okay then, I'll give you a week to get it in. But I'm going to have to take five points away for every day that it's late. If I don't see it in a week, you fail the project."

John groaned. "You'll see it!"

"And that goes for everyone else as well. You've had all semester to work on this. In fact, the last two weeks of class time have been dedicated to working on this project in particular. Remember? I even let you work outside the classroom to do research."

When Mr. Danielson turned around, John mumbled some profanity and gave him the finger.

Seth looked him straight in the eyes. John stared back.

Mr. Danielson pulled a television from the closet in the back of the room. He dragged it up front and plugged in the VCR located on the second shelf of the metal audiovisual cart.

"I thought that since you've all worked hard on your projects, we could sit back and enjoy some of them over the course of the next week. So, I'm going to ask a few of you to read from your essays, we'll check out Justin's Web page, and I was thinking that today we could watch a few of the video essays. But, since Seth was the only participant in the video challenge, we'll at least take a peek at his. Cool?"

"I love movies," commented Cooper, sitting up from his slouching position, "especially ones I'm in." He was proud of his part in Seth's video project. He wanted to take any chance he could to show himself off.

"Oh, a starring role, Cooper?" Mr. Danielson kidded back.

"I'm always the star," Cooper said, confidently standing. He winked at Karissa and blew a kiss in her direction. His lips motioned the word *Tonight*, and he thrust his pelvis a few times. She returned a smile.

"Let me get Seth's tape here," Nick said, digging through the box of projects. He picked up the videotape, placing it into the front of the VCR. "Seth, any comments before we begin?"

Seth thought for a moment and then stood, facing his peers. "Uh, not really. I interviewed most of you in this class at different times and different places. All of the answers were interesting. You'll see. Especially Liz's."

The door clicked shut. Liz made her way to the desk that for an entire semester she had called home.

"Why Liz's?" said Mr. Danielson.

"I don't want to give it away."

"You just want a date for prom," shouted a voice from the back. "So you can get another trophy in your quest for accomplishment."

Seth knew where the voice was coming from. His old friend John.

Mr. Danielson kept the conversation going as he rewound the tape. "And what accomplishment is that, John?"

The class snickered.

"Everyone knows. Prom is all about one thing. Let me give you a hint. Everybody's doing it."

"That's not it!" Seth quickly shot back.

"Oh, just say it," added Cooper. "It's sex."

"It's not about that!" cried Seth defensively. It wasn't that he didn't want sex, but it just wasn't what he was looking for in a relationship anymore. He'd had enough of weekend relationships. All they left was a hole in his heart. He wanted something that was real. Genuine. Deep. He saw that kind of depth in Liz. She had something that he wanted.

Liz looked down at her desk awkwardly. The conversation she'd had with her mother that morning ran through her mind.

"Okay," Nick Danielson said back to his class, "that is enough of that. You can talk about this in your health class. This class is not about the facts of life, but life itself. Okay?"

The class paused.

"Now, let's watch this and talk about your answers to 'the question.' Life has to do with a lot more than just sex. That is why I assigned this project, so you would have to dig deeper than eighteen-year-old minds usually do. And I hope we go deeper than this conversation."

For Nick, life had been deeper. He knew life was so much more than these young minds realized. Just a few years ago, Nick had the kind of life most of these students only dreamed of. He was a well-liked teacher in a posh district in northern California. He worked hard during the week, partied hard on the weekends, and married the girl of his dreams. Shortly after they tied the knot, Tracey found out that she was pregnant. Two weeks later the baby died inside her. Three miscarriages later, Kasey was born prematurely. Nick understood how fragile life was. The party life quickly faded when his and Tracey's dreams fell apart. Just a year ago, shortly after their move to Phoenix, he found himself inside a church one Sunday morning, desperate for an answer. It was there that he found it.

"Okay, Toby, will you hit the lights for us? I present to you, Seth Anderson's 'The Meaning of Life.' Is John Cleese in this?" he joked. No one got it.

The video started rolling. It was dark, but you could hear Seth's voice . . .

"Is this thing on? Still dark. This is crazy. What button am I not pushing? Oh, I guess it helps if you take the lens cap off. Good one, Seth. You're bright. So bright your SAT scores will get you into the special education college of your choice. Enjoy the short bus . . ."

The class started to laugh.

"Good one, Seth. This has quality written all over it," Cooper said sarcastically.

The darkness cut to a hand being waved in front of the camera and then they saw Seth standing in his bedroom, alone.

"I think we're in business. Uh, this is Seth Anderson. Senior at Lincoln High School. I'm 5'9", well built, dark hair, brown eyes, and presently lookin' for a lady. No, this is stupid. Cut! I'll start over."

Darkness again.

"I thought the outtakes came last?" Justin said to the class, who erupted in laughter. Seth started to sweat.

Seth was on the television screen again.

> "Seth Anderson. Senior at Lincoln High School. Senior philosophy class. My senior project is to make a video that answers the question . . . What is the meaning of life? . . . I'm no movie director, but it was either this or a ten-thousand-word essay on the subject. And, well, Mr. Danielson, you know how I am with words. I'm not sure how good this will be because I'm obviously not that great with the lens cap.

The class started to laugh again. They were enjoying Seth's little project so far. He started to relax. Funny was good, even if it hadn't been planned that way. It could help his grade, and he needed all the help he could get. The project continued. This time he was standing in front of his bedroom wall.

> Seth Anderson. Oh, you already know that. Here is my first interview. I have asked the question, "What is the meaning of life?"

The next shot led to a skateboard moving by the camera and then down a cement hill. In the distance you could see several skaters and roller bladers jumping and falling on the concrete. Someone skated into the shot and stopped.

Uh, this is Seth Anderson at the Chandler Skate Park here in Chandler, Arizona. I guess you already know that. I'm standing here with my friend Shawn. Shawn, wave at the camera.

A relaxed Shawn stared into the lens, looking calm and collected. He wasn't waving.

Shawn show us, in your own way, how you would describe the meaning of life.

Shawn jumped on top of his board and skated down the inside of the cement bowl. The camera followed him into the center of the pit and then recorded a jump he had been working on for months. His feet landed on the board. Seth screamed with excitement.

Way to go, dude! Yeah, that is life. Right on!

Shawn rode back toward the camera and into the center of the frame.

So, Shawn, why does that describe the meaning of life to you?

Shawn paused. He flipped his board up into his hands and spoke softly.

Life is just going out and doing it. I just skated down and did it. I'm in complete control here. Do you know how long that trick took me to learn? A long time. But I did it. I didn't need anybody else to do it for me. That's why I like to skate. I can do it on my own terms and push myself as far as I want to go. There's a lot of meaning in that. Right?

Seth started to circle him with the camera. A kid on a scooter nearly hit Seth as he stepped around Shawn. Skaters were skating by on their boards, grinding rails and anything else that was stationary.

Keep talking. Mr. Danielson is going to want more.

Once again, the class laughed. Seth was an undiscovered comedian.

More? Listen, dude, I just showed you my best trick. Take it or leave   that's life.

He turned to skate off, but then reconsidered and spoke.

Okay, Okay, the best way to answer the question is to say some lyrics from the song I wrote Friday night . . . "Life sucks / Or so they say / I'm trying to handle / The easy way / Live my life / Do what I please / Isn't that what puts society at ease? / Get off my case / I'll foot my own bill / But don't be surprised / When I kill."

What's the title of that song, Shawn?

Shawn paused, then spoke. *Responsibility.*

Before Seth could ask him another question, Shawn had already skated away. He turned the camera on himself.

And so the saga continues, "what is the meaning of life?"

CHAPTER 17

MARK CLARABOUGH TRIED TO GET the ticket agent to find an earlier flight than the 5:30 one he was already scheduled on.

"Please! I told you, my daughter is a student at Lincoln High. There has been a shooting there. Arizona. I just want to get home to make sure she's all right."

"Sir, I know. I'm trying here . . . ," the woman said, tapping her fingernails on the keyboard behind the counter. "But that is the only flight to Phoenix this afternoon. There's a flight taxiing on the runway, but it's too late to get on that. They've already pulled away from the gate."

"Well, how about another airline? Can you check them?"

She kept tapping. Her face showed no sign of victory. "We are the earliest."

Mark sighed. Her professionalism was irritating him. This wasn't a good time for her to show her pride in the airline she worked for. He was talking about his daughter here.

"Part of the problem is that most flights to Phoenix happen in the late morning, early afternoon, and evening. All the early afternoon flights are gone."

"But, my daughter . . . she's my only daughter," Mark said. He started to choke up.

"I just don't know." Her nails dug into the keyboard again.

Mark was getting exasperated now. He needed help, not red tape.

"Excuse me," said a man standing behind him dressed in a blue business suit, "I couldn't help but overhear. I am flying to Alaska for business in a few hours. Is there anything I can do to help this man get home faster?"

Tapping, tapping, and more tapping. "I'm just not finding anything."

The man stepped up to the counter. "Let me be a little more clear here. This man does not have the strength to fight with you. His daughter's life is on the line. I'll pay whatever it takes to stop that plane on the runway right now."

"Sir, the issue isn't money here."

"Good, then get on that phone and call someone," he said sternly. "This is a national emergency. The entire country is aware of the shooting."

The ticket agent paused for a moment and then picked up the phone. The man turned to Mark, who had slumped his head onto the agent's check-in desk, and put a hand on his shoulder. "We're doing whatever we can. You have my word."

Mark shook his head in gratitude. He couldn't move. He couldn't talk. Tears fell from his face onto the white Formica countertop. Mark heard the agent hang up the phone. The sound signaled defeat again.

"You're never going to believe this. Because of the situation, they are turning the plane around on the runway and coming back. They are coming back."

Mark looked up now.

"Gate C6. Hurry, they said to hurry."

Mark thanked the man in the blue suit and noticed his pilot's badge. He then turned, grabbed his carry-on bag, and ran through the airport like a maniac. There was no way he was going to miss this flight.

He was escorted somberly through the terminal and onto the plane. The passengers stared at him angrily. For all they knew, he was just an irresponsible businessman who almost missed his flight. For a moment Mark felt a need to address the entire plane, but he knew nobody would understand.

"Sir, there is an empty seat in the third row from the back."

Mark scurried to the back of the plane. He squeezed through the aisle and sat down in a middle seat. The two passengers on either side of him ignored his presence there. He laid his head back on the seat rest and closed his eyes. The jet started to move. Liz, all he could think about was Liz.

"I'm coming, baby . . . ," he whispered to himself. Mark reached for the cell phone in his pocket.

The plane continued to taxi away from the gate. "Please turn off all portable electronic devices including laptop computers, Palm Pilots, radios, CD players, and cell phones."

Cell phones. He put it back in his pocket.

As the plane left the Denver ground, Mark started to sob. The engine noise at takeoff hid his cries. The woman next to him was staring.

"Tough good-bye?" she said politely.

Mark wiped his wet face with his sleeve. "I pray it won't be."

She looked back at him, puzzled.

"I don't want to say good-bye. Not yet."

CHAPTER 18

"So, YOU'RE SAYING THAT THE SHOOTERS began in a west-wing classroom, tore up the hallway, headed to the lunchroom, then shot up the east wing, moving into the auditorium before returning to the same classroom?"

"Yes, that's exactly what I'm saying, and that classroom is where we are heading. It's the focal point of all the killing. Some kind of philosophy class."

"That seems odd to me. Why would they choose to start shooting in a class? How did they get all that artillery inside the school?"

"Well, Dr. Webb, that's the question we're all asking. I think it's logical to assume that they started in the west wing, but I think it is highly unlikely that they could have had that kind of artillery in class."

"Hmm," Duanne said to himself.

"Hmm? Hmm, what?"

"Well," Duanne continued, walking down the shredded hallway, "it seems odd that there is such a large body count in the classroom if these students had time to get away. Is the classroom near an exit?"

"Yes, the west exit."

"That just seems odd to me. But that's for the FBI

to figure out. It's my job to let them know who died and how they died."

Duanne and the lieutenant stopped dead in their tracks. They were standing outside what was left of the classroom door. They stood there silently, stunned at what they saw. "Dear God, that door looks like a bomb hit it."

The door was splintered in every direction. It resembled a toothpick, torn in half and trampled on the ground. A backpack that had been used as a shield lay on the tile, ravaged by bullets. Papers were everywhere. It reminded Duanne of someone taking an industrial fan and turning it on in front of a stack of loose papers. Drops of blood marked the tile floor all the way down the west hallway. The gray walls only added to the feelings both men were experiencing. Duanne closed his eyes for a second, trying to imagine what it must have been like. He thought of the panic, the terror, and worst of all, the fear. He knelt down, staring at the scattered shells.

"Looks like they thought this was one big video game, point and shoot. How many digital hallways and tunnels did they walk down, practicing the skills they used today?"

"Maybe," replied Webb, "but . . . but violence is triggered more by what we experience in life than what we play in a video arcade."

"Well, Doctor, this is it. I wish this were just a video game. This is real. Sickeningly real."

Bill nudged what was left of the door. The hinges squeaked as it opened. A few pieces of wood splintered off the door and fell to the tile.

"Let's get this done, so the forensics team can get in here," Duanne remarked assertively. Dealing with it like it was a job would help him cope with what he would see. He had used this tactic before.

Bill walked into the classroom and covered his nose. "Oh, it smells." The ironlike metallic scent of blood was evident. It was a strong, thick stench.

Duanne had smelled the stench before, every day in fact. He scanned the room. Nielson was right. It was the most grim crime scene he had ever seen. Both men stood frozen. The silence was eerie.

The disorder of the room seemed catastrophic. Duanne couldn't move his feet without coming into contact with a body. Blood had spattered the walls and white board. Small things became the evidence of what the last few minutes of their lives must have been like. An overturned desk with two bullet holes had taken the form of a shield. Duanne noticed a note on the floor; it seemed to mock the grisly scene.

Crystal, let's talk about it after class. I was already late. Mr. Danielson is watching me.

A cool breeze flew through the room, causing the hair on Duanne's arm to stand up and a few tattered papers to blow across the floor. A window looked smashed, maybe by the desk that was now lying on the grass outside. There had been some type of rescue attempt, Duanne reasoned. He wondered if they had made it out safely.

Duanne surveyed a few of the bodies before actually pronouncing them dead. One of the young men lay in a position that resembled someone who had been begging for his life. His hands were folded and his face still had a look of fear. Duanne thought about the fear.

"These kids must have been afraid. Look at them. I can't even imagine."

Lieutenant Nielson was quiet. He had visited this room several times today. His team had been first in the classroom after the gunmen had finished their carnage. When Bill initially entered the room, he remembered feeling that these brilliant young lives had been robbed; life and their youthful innocence had been plundered.

"Can you turn that television off!" Duanne said, irritated.

The screen resembled the white snow you might see after the late-night talk shows were over. The VCR had automatically rewound the tape, but there had been no one there to push play. Investigators would soon find out that the final minutes of the classroom had so very much to do with the tape in the VCR.

"I don't even know where to start. How many in here?"

"Thirteen."

Duanne shrugged. He took another pair of rubber gloves from his pocket. Recording the time of death would be easy, closing their eyes wouldn't be. "Let's just do this."

CHAPTER 19

"BERNICE? CAN YOU HEAR ME? Bernice?" Mary Lou said softly to her friend who was lying on a stretcher at the Red Cross station. They were close to where everything had just taken place.

"Mary Lou? The officer," Bernice said, waking up from the stress and shock. "Where is the officer? Is he all right? And Liz, have they found Liz?"

Mary Lou grabbed Bernice's hand. "Don't worry about that now. We just need you back."

Bernice sat up. "No, I need to know. Has anybody seen Liz?" She was starting to sound angry.

"I don't know. They rushed the officer to the hospital. They rushed you over here. No one has seen Liz. I don't know what is happening, Bernice. I just don't know what is happening!" Mary Lou covered her face with her hands, and she started to sob.

Bernice sat up from the bed, looking around, and reached out for her friend. "I'm sorry. We've got to stick together, Mary Lou. Right now, we're all we've got." Both women leaned on one another, crying for their lost children.

Mark Clarabough dashed off the plane, through Sky Harbor Airport's second terminal and into the parking garage. He paid the attendant and shot out of the garage like a horse in a race. He drove as fast as traffic would allow him. Since it was rush hour now, there wasn't a great deal of mercy for anybody who had an emergency. Mark risked using the diamond lanes for car pools, even though he was the only person in the car. He picked up his cell phone and dialed Bernice's number.

"You've reached the cellular voice mail of Bernice Clarabough. Please leave a message after the beep."

"Bernice," her husband said in a panic, "it's Mark. I'm not sure where you are, but I'm back in Phoenix. I'm on the 202 heading home. I should be there in about twenty minutes. I'll check home first, then drive down to the school. Please call me when you get this message so I can find you and Liz. Bye"

Mark pressed the end button on his phone. He flipped on the radio, trying to dial in a station that was covering the massacre.

"You're listening to KLWZ, Phoenix's number one oldies station, with our news exclusive on the tragedy today at Lincoln High."

Mark turned up the volume.

"Here is the latest news on today's school shooting."

Mark gripped the steering wheel with both hands. He was stuck in traffic. Even if everyone on the freeway wanted to let him pass, it would still be impossible. Things would have to move at their own maddeningly slow pace before Mark could get out of traffic. He hated Phoenix traffic now more than ever.

"C'mon, c'mon!"

"Although the shooting at Lincoln began around the noon hour and stopped over four hours ago, the school is still under a bomb threat. Police have not released any information regarding the number of students who are injured. However, it does appear that there have been a number of student deaths, according to sources at the scene. Local hospitals report that over sixty wounded students have been admitted to emergency centers all over the East Valley. Most of these students have been admitted because of shrapnel or being trampled while trying to get out of the school. A few students are being hospitalized for gunshot wounds. Again, there is no word on how many students have been killed. Maricopa County Coroner, Duanne Webb, was taken out of the building recently due to an explosion in one of the classroom wings. He will resume his work shortly, authorities say."

Mark reached for the radio and scanned the different stations in the area. They all seemed to be saying the same thing. Students were injured, and deaths had occurred. Mark kept listening for Liz's name to be read. He wiped some sweat from his forehead and turned down the volume. He swallowed hard. The thought of Liz being one of those bodies made him sick.

"This seems like some terrible nightmare," he

muttered to himself. "This can't be happening. This can't be happening."

Bernice stood up from the cot, collecting her purse and shoes that were placed to the side of it.

"Ma'am, are you sure you feel ready to leave? Maybe some more rest will ease the tension. Do you have any food in your stomach?" a nearby Red Cross volunteer said.

Bernice flushed with irritation. *Why is it that people say the dumbest things at a time like this,* she thought to herself. "I can't rest. I can't eat. Not until I find my daughter. That's the only thing that will bring me peace. Mary Lou, let's go. Let's try the elementary school. I'm sure Denalyn and Liz are there," Bernice said, rushing out of the Red Cross tent. She looked around, taking in the grim reality.

Things outside the school looked desperate. Although the last shot had been heard hours before, a recent explosion had everyone nervous about the possibility of more bombs in the school. Parents looked worried, and some were crying. Bernice pushed through the crowded street in front of Lincoln High that was lined with policemen, FBI vehicles, news reporters, and a few parents. Mary Lou followed quickly behind her.

"Excuse me, Mrs. Danielson," Bernice said to a familiar face she had seen around the school before, "do you know if all the students are out?"

Mrs. Danielson looked over at Bernice, breaking out of a trance she had seemed to be in. She had been staring at the school. "Uh, I think so."

"I'm Bernice, Bernice Clarabough. Liz's mother? She was a student of your husband's. I've seen you around the school occasionally."

"Oh, sure. I think I know Liz."

"I'm sorry to bother you. But do you know what's happening? I fainted about an hour ago, and I don't have any idea what's going on."

Tracey stuttered through her sentence. "Me, ah, me either. It's . . . well . . . I . . . they say everyone is out. As far as they can tell. There could be more in there hiding, they aren't sure. All of the students were bused to Borsche Elementary. I was there a little while ago. They can't find Nick. He wasn't there. He wasn't there!" she screamed, starting to sob.

Mary Lou and Bernice huddled around her.

"It's just that," Tracey said between her tears, "I left the baby with our neighbor. She's not even off oxygen yet, and Nick, he has to be here somewhere. I can't do this alone. He, ah, he feeds her every night. When she's crying, he's the only one who can get her to sleep. I just don't know what I'm going to do. What am I going to do?"

"Come here," Bernice said, gently taking her in her arms. "Shh. Now, don't you worry about anything. We don't know anything for sure."

A policeman escorted the three women to Bernice's car. It had been blocked in by a CNN truck. A crew of cameramen and techs were working to get the transmitter on top of the vehicle moved in the right direction.

"Go ahead and back up," the Phoenix policeman said, leading her out of the jam the truck had her in. "Now," he continued, leaning his face inside her window, "you ladies check in over at the school. There's no reason to panic; that is where all the kids are waiting. I've sent hundreds of parents over to the school. Go inside to the gym. Unclaimed students are waiting on the stage so that they can keep a record of who is accounted for. It's just three miles away. Drive safe on your way over; no need to rush."

Bernice smiled, rolling up her window. However, she was bursting with irritation in her heart again. "No need to rush? Does *he* have a missing daughter?"

Mark Clarabough ran through the house, calling for Bernice or Liz. Doors were open, the television was on, and closets were open. All signs that Bernice had been there but had left in a hurry. Mark picked up the phone and dialed her cell number.

The phone stuffed inside Bernice's glove compartment started to ring again. The three women had just shut the car doors before rushing inside the elementary school. Mark sighed when the voice mail message picked up. He hung up the receiver and grabbed his keys.

I'm coming, he said to himself. *Bernice and Liz, I'm coming!*

Mary Lou opened the door to the gymnasium. The noise ripped through her ears. Inside the elementary school gymnasium hundreds of people were talking, even screaming. Bernice walked inside with her arm around Tracey.

"They've got to be here. They just do!"

"I hope so!"

A scream ripped through the crowd. A girl on stage started to jump up and down. "Mom, mom! Mary Lou!" the voice shouted.

Mary Lou smiled, starting to cry. "Denalyn!" she screamed back. "Thank God, you're safe, Denalyn!"

Denalyn darted from the stage and out onto the floor. Mary Lou ran through the crowd, pushing several adults and children aside. Their reunion was a sweet one. Both mother and daughter collapsed into one another's arms.

"Mom, I thought you would never get here!"

"I'm sorry, honey," Mary Lou said, wiping her daughter's tears.

"I was with Bernice and well, oh, it's a long story. I'm just glad that you're safe."

Bernice stood with Tracey, scouring the crowd for

her redheaded girl named Liz. It was hard for her to admit it to herself, but Bernice was starting to resent the reunion between Mary Lou and her daughter. This was the reconciliation that Bernice had been dreaming about. She closed her eyes for a second and tried to get back a positive perspective.

"Tracey, I'm going to check on the stage. Can you see if someone has a list of students and teachers that may have been wounded? I'll meet you back here in a few minutes."

Tracey looked at her, frozen.

"Sweetheart, you can do this. We're going to find them," Bernice encouraged her before rushing through the crowd toward the stage.

The adrenaline inside Bernice was pumping now. A knot filled her stomach. She started to breathe hard. It wasn't long before she was starting to scream.

"Liz. Liz Clarabough! Has anybody seen Liz!"

Parents, teachers, and even students stared at her. The room seemed to move into a slow-motion mode.

"Liz. She has red hair. I know some of you know her. Where's my Liz!"

Bernice had reached the point now where something must be done. Lincoln's physical education teacher, Mrs. Wiley, approached her.

"Excuse me, can I help you?"

"I'm looking for my daughter, Liz Clarabough. Senior."

Bernice ran up on the stage while Mrs. Wiley checked the clipboard she was holding.

"Have you seen Liz?" Bernice said to a girl with a

bandage around her head. The girl looked down, shaking her head.

"How about you? Or you? Anybody? Liz Clarabough. She's a senior? Has anybody seen Liz?" Bernice grabbed the shoulders of a young man standing in front of her. "You've got to know where she is. Isn't she here? Isn't she?"

"Mrs. Clarabough! Mrs. Clarabough! Please, these students have been through enough. Let him go. Please, let him go."

Bernice breathed deeply and got ahold of herself. She looked the frightened young man in the face. "Sorry. I'm so sorry."

Mrs. Wiley took Bernice by the shoulder, turning toward her. "Why don't we go sit over here."

The gym teacher led her to a group of chairs located in the corner, close to a pair of locker room doors. The gym seemed to be emptying out now.

"Now, Liz has not checked in yet at this point," she said gently to Bernice. "But that doesn't mean she isn't with a friend or something. Some of the students left with friends after exiting the school. Do you live close by?" she asked.

Bernice shook her head.

"Well, maybe she had a friend did. Many of the students never checked in here. I don't see Liz's name on our hospital list either. But that doesn't mean she isn't there."

"Well," Bernice said quietly, "then where could she be?"

"Mrs. Clarabough, we had over twenty-nine hundred

students in attendance when the bell rang this morning. She could be anywhere. Now, we're suggesting that if you can't find your child that you try any possible leads. Keep checking the hospitals, and if you still can't find her"—she stopped awkwardly, "then . . . then check with the Maricopa Police Department. They will have more information."

Bernice looked up from the floor. "What do you mean? That my child is dead?"

"I didn't say that. They have not identified any bodies yet. Let's believe that your daughter is not inside Lincoln."

"I'm trying."

Mark Clarabough opened the gymnasium doors. The room was emptier than it had been before. He scoured the room for Liz, noticing Bernice sitting on a chair in the left-hand corner.

"Bernice," he said loudly, "Bernice!"

"Mark?"

She rose from her seat, running into his arms. "Oh, I'm so glad you're home. You're here!"

"Where's Liz? Have they found Liz?"

Bernice shook her head, burying her face in his shoulder. "They can't find her," she mumbled, "they can't find her. What do we do, they can't find her!"

"Bernice," Tracey said softly, standing behind Mark. "No record. No record of Liz or Nick. No hospitals report them there."

"Come here," Bernice said gently. Mark and Bernice embraced Tracey. It had been a long day for all of them.

Although they really didn't know one another, that didn't matter. Until they found Nick and Liz, they were family. Through the tragedy, they had become family.

CHAPTER 20

"JANET? HELLO, EARTH TO JANET?" The assistant director of Channel 4's 5:30 broadcast snapped his fingers in front of her face. "Janet!"

"Oh, sorry," she said, coming out of her thoughts.

"You okay?"

"Yeah. I'm doing fine. It's just been quite a day."

"I'll say. You need a cup of water or something? You look like you could use it. We're waiting on John anyway, to go over the day's top stories before the half hour."

"Sure. I'll take some water. Maybe something stronger if you've got it."

The assistant director winked at her, heading out the stage exit door.

Janet couldn't stop thinking about the decision that she had made today. It had been the biggest break in her career. All the "biggies" had been there. CBS, NBC, ABC, MSNBC, and CNN. Each one of them had used a piece of her original footage with Maria that had been taped live earlier that afternoon. CNN even did a story on what it was like for Janet and John to cover such a big event without warning. She sighed; it had been a long day, and the night didn't look any better. It had been hours since the shooting and she still hadn't heard from her son. She figured that he must have gone home with a friend. She had privately called and asked her next-door neighbor to check on the house and, if possible, to head down to the school. *He'll call soon*, she reassured herself, just as she had reassured all the parents who were watching. She started to stare again, remembering the conversation that she'd had over a quick dinner, just a few days ago, with her only boy.

"I know I've been working a lot lately, and I'm sorry. Are you all right?"

"Yes."

"Are you sure? You seem quiet," she said, passing him a bowl of microwaved mashed potatoes.

"Mom, I'm used to this. It's always been this way. Dad left. We moved. You got a job. I go to school. Why wouldn't I be all right? Nothing's changed."

"Well, that's what I mean. Should we change it?"

"You're asking me? I'm not the parent."

She paused. "I thought about having you live with your father next year." She waited for a response, moving the mashed potatoes around on her plate with her fork. "How would you feel about that? The change might do you some good."

Her son's silence made a strong statement. His face flushed red with anger. Even his eyes started to dilate. After a few minutes he responded. "Why?"

"Well, I thought—"

"You thought what?" he said, slamming his fork down on the plate. "So you can work on your big career? I'll be in college; you won't see me much. Besides, send me to live with Dad and I might kill him. I hate him." He pushed his chair away from the table.

"Can we not talk about hate so much?" Janet said, staring directly into his eyes. Even her caring tone couldn't settle him down. She reached over to touch his hand, but he pulled it away.

"Why not? Down deep I know you do, too. You wouldn't be working so hard on your career if you didn't. You're just proving to yourself that he didn't win by leaving you for that witch."

"Hey!"

"It's true."

"It is not! I'm working on my career for us, not him. I'm my own person now. I don't need him, or anyone else for that matter."

"Even God?" he said back sarcastically. The comment took him by surprise.

Where did that come from, she wondered.

"Yes, even God. Now, let's drop the sarcasm, all right?" Janet shot back, standing and starting to clear the table. Dinner was over, and so was the conversation. "It was just a suggestion."

"And a bad one."

She paused again, trying to reason with her son one more time. "So, should I stop working to stay home with you? It is your last year of school."

"Mom, why? Why change something now? I do okay by myself; I don't need you to suddenly do everything for me. Besides, I like being alone."

"You do?" she said, puzzled, picking up his plate.

"Sure. And you like to work. So don't stop. Become the best anchor in town. In the world." He softened, seeing it as the quickest way to get out of the discussion.

Janet smiled. "Then I will," she said, feeling that she had accomplished something. Testing the waters was a part of her parental obligation. She wanted to hear that everything seemed okay, so she could resume her ambition with a clear conscience. As far as she could tell, that had happened. She couldn't wait for her next big story.

"Here's your water, Janet," her assistant director said, startling her from a trance again.

"Oh, thank you."

"You're on in five."

"Where's John?"

"I'm working on that right now."

"After today, John's going to wish he was a woman," she said back, "I will be the best-known anchorwoman in town."

"That you will! We're proud."

"So am I."

"You've worked hard. Has it been worth it?" he echoed back.

Janet paused. "I think so. On a day like today, I'll say, yes."

"Just what I thought. Gotta find John."

Janet laughed to herself. After tonight, things were going to change. A raise, a new location, maybe even an anchor job on one of the networks. She was dreaming while her son was living a nightmare.

CHAPTER 21

SETH PUSHED THE BUTTON next to the front door that signaled inside that someone was waiting on the walkway.

"I'll get it," a sweet voice echoed through the house.

The door clicked and then opened. Seth pushed the record button on the camera, holding the eyepiece up to his face.

"David, tell me, what do you think," he said, stopping midsentence. "Uh, you don't look like David," he continued, staring at her through the eyepiece.

"That's because I'm not," said David's mother. "He's up in his room. I'm his mother. I guess you probably figured that out. Can I tell him who's here?"

"Seth. Seth Anderson. He's helping me out with my philosophy project."

"Oh, that's right. He's been working on that for weeks. What a large paper to write." Her short and frail frame matched the long, thin hair that fell over her shoulders. She was wearing a pair of khaki shorts and a cotton polo shirt.

Seth smiled. Every time somebody said something like that he was relieved to have taken on the video project. "Yes, it is. That's why I'm working on the video project instead. I'm a terrible typist."

"I am, too, but I think David uses three fingers instead of my two. So, he's ahead of both of us. He's been up in his room a lot lately—she gestured to Seth to come in—working on that project. Every night he comes home from school and locks himself in. I don't think I ever had an assignment like that." She paused, then speaking up the stairs, "David! David, someone is here for you!"

No answer.

"I'll be right back. I'm glad you're here. Can I get you something to drink?"

"No, that's okay."

"Well, if you want something it's in the refrigerator. I'm so glad to see he has some friends," she sighed, heading up to the second floor. "Sometimes we wonder."

Seth looked around the front room of the Arizona home. It was decorated in expensive Southwestern paintings and pottery. He couldn't find a trace of dust or dirt anywhere. Everything seemed immaculate. Even the chandelier that hung in the entryway sparkled brightly when the light hit the glass pieces. Seth stepped farther inside, going from the entryway into a room off to the right. A leather couch and marble end table were nestled in the corner. Seth walked inside, staring at the pictures on the walls. He noticed weddings, childhood memories, and David growing up through the years. There were shots of Mom holding him, and shots of Dad fishing with him. Seth looked closer at the pictures, puzzled. There seemed to be another boy in most of them. He had blond hair and blue eyes that glowed.

"The all-American family," Seth grumbled to himself. He wished his own family looked more storybook-like. He wondered why David seemed so quiet if things at home appeared so good. Still, it seemed unusual—a kind of weird wholesomeness.

"There you are," David's mom said from behind.

"Oh, sorry, just looking at the pictures."

"It's funny," she said back, "I clean this room every week, and I rarely look at them anymore. We've all kind of grown up and gone our separate ways."

"I noticed David has a brother, right? I've never seen him."

She paused for a moment, then continued. "He had a younger brother. About ten years ago, David and Corey were out by the pool at our old house, alone, and well, uh, Corey fell in." She stopped again. "David tried to save him, but he couldn't lift him out. By the time I got there, it was too late."

Seth stared down at the ground. He felt awkward. "I'm, uh, very sorry."

"I am, too. It's been hard on him. He doesn't talk about it much. That's why it's good that you came over. We don't have many visitors."

Seth looked in a different direction. He didn't have the heart to tell her that the only reason he was there was to finish his video project. He only had a few people left in his class to interview, and David was one of them.

"Well, it's good to be here."

"Stay as long as you like. David's up in his room waiting. Just head up the stairs. First door on your right."

Seth walked quietly out of the room and headed up the staircase. He held on to his camera tightly. Just a quick interview would do. Then he was gone. This place was starting to make him feel uncomfortable. He knocked on the door.

"Come in," David said quietly.

Seth nudged the half-open door and walked in. "Hey, David. How's it going?"

David was sitting at his computer. Seth noticed that he was on the Internet studying information on a Web page.

"Oh, hi," David said back.

"What are you doing?" Seth said, walking up behind him.

"Research."

"What kind? For your paper? I know how much it means to you," Seth said sarcastically.

"No, just research."

Seth tried to notice what Web page David was on, but he closed the window before Seth could focus. "Listen, I won't take up much of your time. I just need a few more interviews, with the project being due next week and all."

"Yeah, I haven't even started mine."

"What?"

"I don't care. I'm considering not even doing one."

"Why? Don't you want to graduate?"

David was silent. Seth felt a little awkward.

"Sure I want to graduate. But I'm tired of jumping through everybody's hoops just so I can."

Seth put down the camera, sitting on the end of David's bed. "But isn't that life?"

"I guess. But I have the choice to do what I want with it."

"So, is that your meaning of life? Should I be taping this?"

David turned around from the computer. "I don't know."

"Dude, what is up with you lately?"

"What?"

"I don't know. Just listening to you tonight. Or the way you look lately. You just seem different."

David looked down at the carpet. "Uh, I don't know. I guess I'm just tired of living silent."

"Your mom told me about your brother."

"So?" David said defensively.

"I just wondered if maybe that had something to do with it."

David turned back around and started typing something on his computer. "Happened a long time ago. Doesn't bother me. Not everything has to do with that. We're all fine. Let's get this interview done. Just let me log off here."

Seth wanted to get the interview done, too. This was by far one of the hardest moments in the project. With just a week left to finish, he was starting to notice a pattern in the people he interviewed. Very few of them really seemed to be happy at all. Most of them just seemed to be surviving, barely living. *Why?* he wondered. It was like everybody was depressed, or angry, or hopeless. He wished all of that was currently out of fashion, but some things are classic.

Seth looked around David's room. A lava lamp pumped goop around the glass inside, rotating it round and round. A few skate-punk posters decorated the walls. The room seemed dark, discouraging, even depressing. A car calendar with a couple of blonde chicks lying on the hood was tacked up next to his door. Large, red X's counted down the days in May. Even today had already been marked.

"You counting down to graduation? Me, too."

No response. David turned around, acting as if nothing had been said.

"Okay, ready. Let's just get this done."

"All right. Let me see here," Seth said, picking up the camera from the bed and turning it on. "I'll get this focused." He held the camera up, looked through the viewfinder, and hit the record button. "All right, David, can you tell me what, in your own words, is the meaning of life?"

David paused before turning toward the camera in his desk chair. "Meaning of life," he said, rubbing his chin in affected contemplation. "Meaning of life. I don't know. Ah, the question that keeps running through my mind lately. I say back to you, 'Is there a meaning to life?' I used to think there was. But after a great deal of careful research and study that a friend and I have been doing, we've come to the conclusion that life basically sucks."

Seth's stomach started to turn. He needed something real for Mr. Danielson, not this crap.

"And there is no way out of it. It's like a prison, and no matter how may times you try to break out, you always wind up back in. So, I guess you could say you're stuck in it. That's why it sucks."

Seth asked a question. "What in your life has brought you to that conclusion?"

David thought for a moment and then rose from his desk chair. Seth followed David with the camera. He walked over to a shelf that sat next to his bed. He grabbed something off it and held it directly in front of the camera. Seth focused in on it. A small, worn, blue metal Matchbox car sat in the palm of David's hand.

"It belonged to my brother. He drowned. I tried to save him."

David reached up, pushing the record button off.

"Hey, what did you do that for?"

"I was done."

"It was just getting good!"

"Why is that?"

"Because, because you were finally getting to what makes life suck for you. I think I'm starting to understand."

"You don't understand any of it. Besides, did you come over to counsel or film me?"

"All right, I'm going."

"Well, go get an A for me then."

Seth shut off the camera, holding it by the handle at his side.

"See you."

David nodded, turned around, and headed back to his computer.

CHAPTER 22

MR. DANIELSON PUSHED PAUSE on the VCR remote.

"Toby, can you get the lights?"

Toby reached for the light switch. Everybody's eyes squinted when the fluorescent bulbs kicked in.

"A good start for us. I think we are getting somewhere. If nothing else, Seth, your video helps us to see that each one of us answers that question in a different way. Everybody's perspective is different. Karissa, why don't you share what you think the meaning of life is?"

He had caught her off guard. She was in the middle of writing a note to Crystal about the party she had been to on Friday night. Crystal had gotten into a situation with a guy they both knew that made her very uncomfortable. He had forced her to do some things that she had never done, despite the woman of experience she pretended to be.

"Karissa? Can you put the note away and share in the discussion with us?"

"What?"

"Your report?"

Karissa laughed nervously. "Um, I don't know?"

Mr. Danielson set the marker he was using on the white board down on his desk. He sighed. "You don't? You just wrote ten thousand words on it."

Karissa teased back. "I know that! I wrote a report, I promise! I just don't know what I should say."

"Then let me help you. Why don't you find your paper and share a paragraph from it with us?"

Karissa didn't like this. She liked attention in class, but read from her report? It might show how incomplete her assignment really was. Mr. Danielson nodded his head again.

"All right," she replied reluctantly, folding the note and sticking it into her pocket. She made her way to Mr. Danielson's desk and dug through the box. The class seemed disinterested and started to talk.

"Let's hurry, Karissa. Time is ticking away."

Karissa noticed the blue notebook cover and grabbed it out of the box. She thumbed through her report, glancing often at Mr. Danielson. "Do I just read from anywhere?"

Mr. Danielson nodded his head. He couldn't wait to hear what she was going to say.

Karissa flipped to a certain page and cleared her throat. "Well, my good friend Crystal and I—hi, Crystal," she said, waving in Crystal's direction.

Crystal waved back.

Karissa continued on, "I believe that life is all about relationships."

The class started to moan. Liz rolled her eyes. Cooper smiled big.

Karissa found a spot and started to read. "The meaning of life can best be described by the present person you are seeing or dating." She stopped and winked at Cooper. Word around Lincoln was that they were dating again. After the fight a few weeks back at Cooper's party, they had decided to call it quits for a while. They both wanted the option to date other people. But a few days had been long enough. "For that person holds the key to the most important part of life, love."

Liz rolled her eyes. Karissa really bothered her. Liz could never figure out why she tried so hard.

Karissa laughed a little, trying to flirt with Mr. Danielson. She needed an A on this project or she could flunk the class. "Without love, life wouldn't have any meaning."

"Very profound," Nick remarked. "Go on, Karissa."

"Love becomes very important to your definition of life, especially when you've never really understood what it truly is," she said, seriously now. "A new relationship can redefine what your past experience with love has been." Although Karissa was reading from her report, her mind was far away from the words that she had written on the page.

"No, Daddy!" a little girl screamed, running down the hall. "NO! Please, no!"

The little girl's feet transformed, getting a few sizes bigger. Now it was Karissa running down the hall. She, too, was screaming. "No, Daddy. No more!"

She reached for her door handle, twisting it with fear. The door opened violently. She slammed it shut, running to her bed.

"No, please. Not tonight!"

Heavy pounding soon thundered on the door. The sound made Karissa shriek. She knew what her father wanted. It was the same thing he had wanted many times before.

"Go away. I'm too old now, Daddy."

The pounding continued. She felt like an animal. There was nowhere to go, nowhere to hide. The scent of his cologne would be all over her again.

"Please go away. I'll do anything if you'll just go away!"

The shame was coming again. She was feeling it now every day. If anybody knew, she would have died. This was a secret she couldn't tell. But tonight she wanted to tell somebody. Maybe then it would stop. Maybe then her father would go away.

The pounding was getting louder now. It wouldn't be long before he would make his way into her room. She grabbed her pillow and held on to it. She started to cry. "No, I can't do it. I can't. I CAN'T! This isn't love. This isn't real love!"

The door lock had been broken now. Karissa's bedroom door cracked open. Through her tearstained eyes she saw the shadow of her father. A shadow she wished would go away. A shadow that seemed to darken her world forever.

"Daddy, please go away."

Karissa continued to read from her report. "So if you haven't found much meaning in life in the past, there is always the future. Right?" She turned and winked at Cooper.

Cooper gave her a round of applause. "Go, girl. C'mon!"

Mr. Danielson looked sadly at her. It didn't take a rocket scientist to figure out what was behind the black words that she had just read. He decided that he was going to talk to her after class today. If he missed another day, he might miss the opportunity of a lifetime. He could see the desperation in her eyes, and only one thing could fill that, a relationship with Jesus Christ.

"Thanks, Karissa, and, you're right. Our meaning of life is many times shaped by the past. Does anybody identify with that?"

A few hands went up around the room. Nick knew that if everybody was honest with themselves, all the hands would have been up. The past. It had shaped more of these students than they ever wanted to admit. Nick had most of these students only a handful of hours each week. But so much of their behavior came from what they experienced at home. He silently prayed, *Lord, give each one of them a home that is good for them.*

CHAPTER 23

THE PARTY WAS OVER. Seth kicked over a beer can pyramid that was in his way as he headed out the sliding glass door that led him to Cooper's backyard. Even with the door closed, he could hear the music still blaring from the living room stereo. "Cooper?" he said quietly.

He heard a noise and noticed a couple making out under the patio table.

"Cooper?" Seth said. He squinted his eyes and looked closer. "Nope, not his type." As if Cooper had a type.

Brett Handel, Lincoln's junior class president, had just thrown up over in the bushes. He was now lying across the patio floor with his face pressed against the cool cement. Two unidentified girls were holding their stomachs as they lay on the trampoline; before long they would be in the bushes, too.

"That's why I don't drink," he repeated twice, then smiling, "at least most of the time."

The deep blue pool light reflected on the cinder-block back wall, projecting a sense of calm that was in marked contrast to the party. Seth put his camera down, took off his shoes, and put his feet in the water.

"Ahhh," he said. It had been a long day, not to mention a long party. Two girls had made him dance. Cooper had grabbed the camera and recorded him dancing. Seth thought about what a moron he had felt like. But seeing Brett Handel puke in the bushes helped him to not feel so bad. As he looked around, it suddenly occurred to him that he didn't really want to be there. Seth stared into the calm waters. Partying didn't always make sense to him.

He noticed a beer bottle floating in the water.

"Seth?" a drunken voice echoed from the shadows by the pump.

"Cooper? Cooper, is that you?"

"Let me check. Yep, it's me." He followed with a big burp. "Ooh, a wet one."

Seth picked up his camera and headed toward the deep end. Cooper was sitting there by himself.

"So what's the host doing out here all by himself?" Seth said. He sat next to Cooper, whose feet were in the water. Seth dropped his in.

"What?" Cooper replied, then laughed to himself.

"The party? Shouldn't you be in the house, saying good-bye or something?"

"Not much of a host, am I!" he replied with the giggles.

Seth wondered how much beer Cooper had drunk. Cooper's breath reeked when he talked. Seth wasn't impressed. In his mind, drinking to the point of foolishness didn't seem like a great time.

"Isn't this kind of dangerous? You know, a drunk

dude sitting next to a pool? Can you spell d-e-a-t-h? If you're not careful you'll end up on News 4."

"Maybe I want to die," Cooper said, smiling, yet sounding serious.

Seth was puzzled. From Seth's perspective, Cooper was the "king" of the school. He was the star quarterback on Lincoln's state championship team, not to mention an all-American basketball player and the school's four-hundred-meter track-and-field record holder. And the girls—Seth couldn't believe how many girls wanted to be with him. Cooper seemed to cast a spell on people wherever he went. Everything he touched turned to gold. Teachers loved him, the school crowned him, and everyone in the community knew who Cooper Severs was. Especially Seth. He had taken many pictures of Cooper for articles written in *THE VOICE*, Lincoln's school newspaper. Seth resented Cooper's self-pity. This guy was popular, well liked, and talented. His problems didn't seem to supersede the reputation that he worked so hard to keep.

"Great party," Seth remarked, changing the subject.

"Yeah, sure. It was good, right?"

Seth felt awkward seeing Cooper like this, really awkward. Never in his dreams did he think Cooper would act this way. He was usually at the center of things. Finding him alone with his feet in the pool didn't exactly fit Cooper's personality.

On a whim, Seth turned on the video camera. He put the camera on his lap, holding the lens up a few inches to capture Cooper's face. He didn't know how Cooper would respond.

"So, Cooper, this seems strange to me. You know, finding you alone out here. This isn't the Cooper we know and love. Dude, what's up?"

Cooper stirred his feet in the water. He didn't answer for a while. Seth was beginning to wonder if Cooper was too drunk to notice that the camera was on.

"You know what, Seth?" he replied slowly, almost lethargically. "This is off the record, by the way. You'd better not put this in your project or I'll beat the heck out of you.

"You asked me what the meaning of life was? That was you, right?"

Seth nodded his head.

"This is the only way I know how to handle it sometimes."

"What?"

"To party."

Seth was trying to make sense of what Cooper was saying. He wondered if Cooper was being honest or just plain drunk.

"You know why I threw this big party tonight anyway?"

"Why?"

"My rich, snobby, 'I don't care about anything but myself' parents told me they're getting a divorce today." Cooper was being honest.

Seth looked away. Now he really was uncomfortable. He didn't like that word. *Divorce.* It reminded him too much of his own life.

"Seth dear, Mommy and Daddy don't love each other anymore."

"Why, Mommy?"

"Because, we just don't. I know that it's hard for you to understand, but you need to try. Daddy isn't going to live here anymore."

"When is he coming back?" Even though he was three, Seth still remembered this moment. He remembered feeling the weight of his tears as they started to tumble from his eyes.

"Seth honey, Daddy isn't coming back."

"You mean I'll never see him again?"

"Not if I can help it."

"But Mommy, I love Daddy."

"I know, honey, but Mommy doesn't. Daddy was very mean to Mommy."

A younger Seth started to wail. "But Mommy, please. Don't let Daddy go. Don't let Daddy go!"

Cooper took a sip of beer from a bottle nearby.

"Oh, I, uh, I'm sorry, Coop. That sucks."

"Yeah, it does. Life sucks. That's why I'm throwing a party. Because the music, the girls, this beer," he said, holding the half-empty beer bottle, "it makes me forget about it for a little while. All the crap. And at least life doesn't seem so real. Is this real? Are you real? Is this water real?" Cooper screamed, tossing the bottle into the middle of the pool. Some water splashed on Seth's lens.

"I, uh," Seth tried to say, but he couldn't recover. He didn't have any answers for Cooper.

Cooper started to laugh uncontrollably. Seth tried to laugh with him. It wasn't long before the drops of water started to roll down Cooper's cheeks. The laughter was turning into cries. Seth pushed the record button to the off position. This wasn't for anyone to see. He awkwardly put his arm around Cooper, who laid his head on Seth's shoulder, sobbing. Seth's hands were starting to sweat. *Will Cooper even remember this?* he thought. Tomorrow things would be back to normal. But for tonight, the party really was over.

CHAPTER 24

"JOHN?"

Still, no response.

"John, are you with us?"

The stare on John's face seemed like a trance. The class was staring now. On most days their participating skills were down, but today most of the class seemed on the upswing. Except for John, that is.

"Hello? Earth to John?" Karissa remarked from a few chairs away. John was getting tired of her. She was constantly picking at him. Everything from his hair to his basic wardrobe of a T-shirt and jeans. He was ready for her to be quiet, permanently.

Mr. Danielson tried again. "John?"

John looked up. Apparently, he was back. "What?" he said with confusion.

"We were just wondering if you were with us? I had asked you a question."

John was getting irritated now. Why didn't Mr. Danielson call on someone else? He didn't want to answer any questions, especially regarding the subject of life.

Mr. Danielson walked closer to where he was seated. "John, what do you think?"

"About what?" he said back with frustration.

"About the past? About how our past shapes our future."

Now John was really irritated. He didn't want to think about the past. Talking about it only made the frustration he felt even stronger. "The past? I think it sucks that somebody else's meaning of life can screw yours up." John leaned back in his seat and folded his arms.

"Talk that out more," his teacher encouraged, seeing an opportunity to get John to open up. John didn't quite view it that way. The class was quiet now. A few students were staring in his direction.

"No comment. I have no comment. There are some things that I don't want to remember."

John was starting to stare again.

"John! John! Let's go. Get your butt down here!"

Jerry Theisen pounded the coffee table that was sitting in front of him. Scattered across it were a few folders, school assignments, some pens, and a pencil. Jerry ran his hand across the mess, knocking it to the floor.

"What?" replied John, coming into the family room of the parsonage that the church had given them. "What, Dad?"

Jerry stood and hollered. "Didn't I tell you to clean up all this crap? Huh?"

He grabbed a few pages of a school assignment, crumpled them up, and threw them at John's chest. They bounced off him, landing on the floor.

"But Dad, it's my homework. I wasn't done with it yet."

"I don't care if you were writing a letter to the president. When I tell you to clean up your crap, you do it, all right?" He paused, then continued. "All right?"

John didn't respond. He stepped back, noticing his father's rage was stronger than normal.

"Don't back away from me!" Jerry screamed, grabbing John by the collar. Jerry pulled John close to his face.

John took a deep breath. Alcohol—he smelled alcohol again. "Dad, let go. I didn't do anything. Let go! You've been drinking again, haven't you?"

Jerry released his son's collar. John fell to the floor. The room was silent for a moment. Jerry's face flushed, turning red.

"C'mon, Dad, what are people in the church going to say?"

John's father came unleashed. Before John could stand, Jerry pounced on top of him. He wrapped his fingers around John's neck. "Does it matter?" he said into John's ear.

John could feel the spray from his father's words on his cheek. He swallowed hard, trying to breathe.

"If you say anything, you'll regret it. And I mean that. I am a pastor and you won't ruin that. You hear?"

"Pastor?" John was able to belt out. "Why do you even bother?"

Jerry let go, slapping his son in the face. "Have I made myself clear?"

He had. John knew it wasn't his fault. The pressures of the ministry and his father's struggle with alcohol were the culprits. John just always seemed to be the punching bag. A tear ran down his cheek. Partly from the pain and partly from the hurt he felt down inside his heart. "Yes," he replied quietly. "Whatever you say, Dad. Whatever you say."

The class was laughing again. John hated this.

"John," Mr. Danielson said, "what is on your mind today?"

John made a fist with his left hand. "Nothing."

"Well, then stay with us, will you? You haven't been with the class at all today."

Mr. Danielson turned around to write something on the board. John flipped him off. But it wasn't just Nick Danielson he was flipping off; in John's eyes it was the whole world. Nothing mattered. The hurt was too deep. Hatred had grown in the same soil that love once had. Love would never grow again.

CHAPTER 25

SETH PARKED HIS 1985 TOYOTA CELICA behind the brick wall that surrounded the upper-class neighborhood in Gilbert, Arizona. He checked the map John had drawn out for him on the back of an old philosophy assignment.

"This looks right," Seth said to himself, referring to his location on the map. He looked around outside his window. *Why would John want me to meet him here?* he thought. The brick wall he parked be-side separated the neighborhood from the desert. All Seth could see was a few rock formations in the distance and a lot of sandy dirt in between.

Seth opened his car door and stepped out. He heard a tin clanking noise in the distance. After grabbing his camera case he locked the doors and headed in the direction of the only sign of life.

He heard another clank, then another. It reminded him of how much he used to enjoy kicking around his dad's empty beer cans as a kid. He turned the corner and started to walk down another outside wall. Just a few yards away he saw John, with a gun in his hand.

"John, John! It's Seth!"

Seth waved. John didn't wave back. Seth noticed that John didn't even look.

"Hey, John. Why the heck did you have me meet you all the way out here? Your house is just a few blocks away, right?"

Still no reply.

"What's the gun for?" Seth insisted on knowing before walking any closer.

"Practice," John replied firmly.

"I hope not on me," Seth said, walking closer.

John shot a BB at a tin can on top of a bucket that had been turned upside down a few yards in front of him.

Seth felt strange. Not so much about where they were meeting, but how John was acting. He took his video camera from its case. "Uh, I really appreciate you doing this, John. You are my last interview. I've only got a few days to get this thing together. You almost done with your project?"

"I've been done for a while."

Seth continued to get his camera ready. "Really. Well then you're a lot more organized than me."

John shot another tin can off the bucket.

"You've got a pretty good aim," Seth replied, focusing his camera on John's face.

"Practice makes perfect."

Seth wondered why John was practicing. "Okay, let's get this over with. I've got about two days worth of editing left to do."

John looked Seth in the eye for the first time since they had been together. "Seth, I've got one favor to ask if I do this for you."

"Name it."

"I want my interview to go last when you show it in class next week."

Seth pulled down the camera, puzzled. "Why?"

"Just because."

Seth thought for a moment and then complied. "Uh, Okay, I guess that could work. No big deal, right? You got it. Your interview will be last. So, give me a great interview."

John turned back toward the cans and continued to shoot.

Seth pushed the record button to the on position. "I am here with senior John Theisen at a secret location somewhere in the Arizona desert." Seth turned the camera toward his face for a moment. "It's really just a few miles outside the city. In fact, right by his house." He focused the shot back on John. "Uh, a little puzzled why John insisted on doing his interview out here, but it must have something to do with target practice. Right, John?" Seth focused the camera on John, who didn't respond, then on the tin cans. "Okay, this is going to be a fun one. So, John, how does this represent the meaning of life?"

John was deliberate in his response. "Watch this," he said, focusing on another can set on the bucket.

Seth zoomed in on the beer can that already had several holes in it. It toppled over soon after it was hit, landing on a pile of cans that had been hit also.

"And?" Seth said back, confused.

John aimed at the cans again and spoke. "Sometimes the way you deal with life doesn't have any meaning. Life screws you so bad that you are forced to control it before it controls you."

"What in life has screwed you up, John?" Seth questioned back like a reporter.

John shot down another tin can.

John paused, then spoke. "People."

Seth wasn't going to let this one go easily. Even though it was odd, it was honest. He continued to dig. "Like, random people? I'm not getting it."

"That's the problem, no one seems to get it. But there is coming a day when everybody will."

"Will what?"

"Get it." John shot down the last can when he answered and walked down to set up the targets again. Seth walked with him, continuing to record.

"Oh, okay. Whatever," Seth replied back to John. "You okay, John?"

"I'm fine," he replied as he finished setting up the cans, then walked back to where he was shooting from before.

Seth followed closely behind him, recording every moment both spoken and silent.

John spoke again, aiming at the tin targets. "I have two messages for some people in my life regarding the meaning of life."

Seth was happy. At least someone was talking about the question Mr. Danielson requested that they answer. This could help him get an even better grade. "okay, go on."

Seth focused the camera on John, who was working intently on his aim.

John spoke firmly, without any emotion. "Mom, this is for you." Seth focused on another perfect shot that knocked down a soda can. "I hope your meaning in life goes far deeper than your stupid career. This is for all the nights you weren't home."

John cocked the gun, aimed at another can, and took it down.

"Dad, this is for you. Thanks for teaching me that other people's choices do affect your life. Your life is screwed up, and so is mine." He paused, staring at the cans. "God, so is mine."

Another can hit the ground with a clank. Seth was focusing on the cans when he noticed the barrel of the gun moving toward the center of the lens, directly in his face.

Seth flinched, but before he could say a word John was already speaking directly into the camera.

"And this is for all of you. Because my life has no meaning, neither will the end of yours!"

CHAPTER 26

LIZ WATCHED THE BLOOD pour from the wound in the lower part of her chest. The initial shock was gone now. She was in a great deal of pain. The crimson puddle on the floor reminded her of an accident that she'd had as a child. She had fallen off her bike onto some loose gravel on the shoulder of the road and had gotten a nasty cut on her forehead. This gave her an L-shaped scar by her eyebrow that Seth had once called "cute." Ten years later her blood was pouring again. It was hard to breathe. It hurt so much that she only did what she had to. When she did breathe it rasped, like pneumonia, and it felt wet. She could taste blood in her mouth. She tried to lay lifeless on the cold floor, in case the killers came back.

A few students that were still alive started to talk to one another.

"Where's Crystal? Crystal?"

"Here, I'm over here!" Crystal shrieked from where she was hiding under a desk. "I can't believe this. Was that John? Why is he doing this?"

"Who's been shot?" Mr. Danielson questioned the class with a tense tone.

"I think Liz was shot right away," Justin said back.

Echoes of a round of shots firing could be heard down the hallway.

"Do you see them?"

"Shhh."

"There is blood everywhere."

Liz tried to say something but nothing would come out. She wasn't worried about herself right now. It was Seth she couldn't stop thinking about. His body lay under hers. She could hear him breathing, but he still wasn't conscious.

"Seth," she tried to whisper. Still, nothing came out. There were so many things she wanted to say. She now possessed that odd single-mindedness that comes from trauma. She wanted to tell him how important he was in the eyes of Christ. She wanted to say that her relationship with God was real. She loved Him with everything she had. Liz really loved the Lord.

Job, she thought. *Oh, Job, I understand.* Her mind went to the character in the Old Testament who lost everything he had, yet still said he would serve God.

"Though He slay me, yet I will serve Him."

She was serving Him. Her body had protected Seth's very life, not to mention giving him another chance to say yes to Christ. She had served Him in her school and made a difference on her campus. And she had served Him by giving her life to Jesus when she felt as if it didn't matter at all.

Liz tried to hum a chorus, even though no sound came out. Even still, it was strong and beautiful as it poured out to the Lord. The words ran through her mind. She had sung it at a youth group meeting just a few days ago.

> *Over the mountains and the seas.*
> *Your river runs with love for me.*
> *And I will open up my heart,*
> *And let the Healer set me free.*

She started to sing the chorus. *I could sing of Your love forever . . .*

Her eyes were heavy now. She kept humming the song. Louder and louder. It sounded like wet gasps to others, but she didn't care. It was all she had to hold on to. It didn't matter what others thought; at this point it just didn't matter. She touched the blood that had now formed a puddle on the floor. Her life was trickling out of her and she knew it. There wasn't much time left. Time. She had written an entry about it in her journal two nights ago:

None of us are promised every day. I know that I am not. In fact, I feel weird right now. I almost feel like my time could be up on any given day. That is why I can't waste one moment. I can't waste one day. I can't believe I used to live such a wasted life. How will my school, my friends, or even Seth be changed, if I don't take every second to live for You, God? If I were to take one second of my life and not care to live for You for that moment; that could be the time that someone is watching.

And someone was watching her. Seth's eyes opened. They looked glazed. He was in shock.

"Seth?" she said. It hurt.

"Shhh," a wounded student signaled back.

"Liz, what happened? Where am I?"

Liz rolled off his body. The pain was excruciating. More than she had ever known. Seth noticed a pool of blood on the floor beside his head.

"I'm bleeding!" he stated, shocked.

"No."

"What?"

Seth noticed the bloody shirt Liz was wearing.

"You?"

"Don't you remember?" Liz tried to say through raspy breaths. "We fell, floor, you hit your head on the tile, unconscious. I fell on you. Somebody asked me if I loved God. I said yes. I was shot in my chest. Seth, I've been shot."

Seth sat up, looking closer at the blood oozing from Liz's body.

"This can't be happening. This can't be happening. We've got to get you out of here."

Seth looked around and noticed two students trying to open a window. Gunshots could be heard echoing in the background. The only way out was the door, which looked like a wafer board from the shots it endured.

"There's got to be a way."

Shawn brushed off the glass from the fluorescent light that was blown out above him. He walked cautiously over to the doorway, peeking out into the hallway. Most of the students were still on the floor, dazed from the sheer unreality of their situation.

"Do you see them?"

"Can we get out of here?"

"I thought I heard sirens."

Karissa started to weep. Her sobs rang through the classroom.

"Somebody shut her up. It's going to make them come back."

Liz took a deep breath. "Seth, it really hurts now."

He knelt beside her. "There's got to be something we can do."

"I know."

"What?" he said back.

"Pray."

"What? What?"

"Seth, I want to see you on the other side," she was able to muster out. The pain was unbearable. Her breaths were getting shallower now.

"I want to see you."

"But Jesus wants to see you there. I can almost feel His arms around me. Ready to take me away."

"No. You're going to make it."

"You've got to make a decision. This is your time."

"But, I'm not ready."

Liz tried to sit up. She fell back onto the floor realizing that sitting wasn't an option. She poured her life into her words. "Seth, what if they ask you? What are you going to say? You've got to make a decision."

Seth was starting to sweat. The air-conditioning had stopped. The room temperature was starting to rise.

"I don't know, Liz. I don't know."

"Yes you do. You've heard all the answers. You've got to come up with your own conclusion. You're going to say yes or no about wanting God in your life."

"They're coming back!" Shawn yelled out.

Shots could be heard hitting the hallway walls and lockers. You could hear laughter coming from where the bullets were being sprayed.

No one was ready for this. How could you be? Seth wondered if he should play dead or not.

"Oh my God, they're almost here."

Shawn ran back to his seat and dropped to the floor. The shattered glass cut into his cheek when he laid his head back on the tile.

"Get down, Seth. I'll get back on top. Get down."

"No, they are not going to do this to any of us."

"Then plan on dying."

The class got quiet.

The hinges that kept the door in the frame squeaked. Combat boots stepped into the bloody room. The footsteps moved over the shattered glass, scattered papers, and shreds of ceiling tile pieces. The room was quiet. All that could be heard now was a few heavy breaths every now and then from Liz, who was struggling to breathe.

"I thought we had finished everyone off," John

said to David, who now entered the room. "Some of them are still breathing." He laughed to himself.

The smell of exposed flesh and blood reeked in the air. David stepped inside the room and stared. Things were starting to feel real now. The grim reality of what he was involved with was starting to kick in. For an hour now nothing had bothered him. Even when he shot one of his best friends in the cafeteria. But something about this classroom did. Maybe it was seeing how helpless everybody seemed now. There was no one left to chase. The game wasn't very much fun anymore. For a brief moment he second-guessed what he had done. "Let's just get this thing over," he said.

"What? Over? Until all of them are dead, nothing is over. We still have some torturing to do. I haven't seen enough blood," John said, smiling, "or even somebody's brain."

John fired a round of shots at Justin's head. "There we go. Cool."

"What did you do that for?" David said, questioning John's actions.

"Because he was alive."

John pointed the gun at David.

"What's up with you? Do you think we can just walk out of this school and surrender, get on a bus and go home? It's not going to happen. This thing is us. We did it. Look at the blood. We shed it. So let's just finish the job and end it."

"We did finish it."

"You're a liar. You said you wanted the whole school to go down. We barely hit anybody. Ten to fifteen kids. So much for target practice. But we did mess up the school. Yes! We messed up this school!"

Sweat drops fell to the floor from David's brow. He felt as if he was going to faint.

"I said we were done. C'mon, John, give it up. You've got your vengeance. Let it go."

"Not until every person I hate is dead." John walked over to Liz, picking her up by the hair.

"So, Liz. You going to witness to me now? Where's your God? If He's real, then why are you bleeding to death?"

"Put her down, John."

"Why? I thought she was already dead."

Liz opened her mouth, but nothing came out.

"You trying to say something?" John sneered with sarcasm.

She tried again. Still nothing. Her lungs were filling with blood. It took all she had just to focus on her thoughts. Liz gasped for air, coughing blood onto the floor. She opened her mouth again to try. "I . . . I . . . I forgive you."

David started to cry.

John threw her on the floor. "Well, I don't forgive you." He pulled his finger on the trigger and shot a round into her back. The room froze. Seth jumped up, trying to grab the gun from John's hands.

"You will not win!" Seth screamed.

John's feet slipped on the glass, and he fell to the floor. Seth jumped on top of him.

"Shoot him! David, just shoot the mother!"

David couldn't move. He had killed enough people.

Seth and John rolled into Justin's body. Some of Justin's blood soaked into the back of Seth's shirt. Seth reached for John's gun. It slid across the floor in David's direction. Seth reached for it, coming up short. John rolled on top of Seth and pinned him to the ground. John planted himself on Seth's back, grabbing a handful of his hair.

"What's your problem, Anderson? Trying to take the glory from me? No way. This is my deal. This is my plan. And no one, not you or anyone in this school, is going to stop it. The world will know after today who I am and will carry my scars throughout history. People will study me; newspapers will put my picture on the front page. For all I know they might even make a movie. And you, you won't stop them."

John smashed Seth's face into a pile of glass on the floor. "So tell me, Anderson, why pull this little high jink? I probably would have left you alone. I knew you weren't dead. But you didn't matter anyway. You've never stood for anything for as long as I can remember. You're no different from me now, are you? Are you?"

"Yes I am!" Seth screamed out loud.

"What? Now you're different? David, you think he's different? Well, do you? I guess I'll have to finish him off now, won't I?" John pulled another gun from his holster, holding it up to Seth's head.

David just stood and stared.

"So, what's the problem, Anderson? You a Christian now? Huh?" John tightened the grip on Seth's hair, pulling his head back. "You'd better say no. You'd better say no, 'cause if you don't, I'll shoot your brains out like Justin's. Are you a Christian? Can't you hear me? I said, 'Are you a Christian!'"

John cocked the gun with his right hand. He pushed Seth's head onto the floor again with his left. Seth tried to breathe but was left with a few short heaves here and there.

John asked him point-blank again, with sarcasm this time. "Do you really want to follow God?"

Seth was quiet. He was at the point of decision. Liz told him he would be here. He remembered what she had said to him.

. . . You've heard all the answers. You've got to come up with your own conclusion. You're going to say yes or no about wanting God in your life."

John yelled in his ear one more time. "Are you a Christian?"

If the clock of time could have stopped, it would have. Another soul, another life, was at the ever-important place of choice. This time, there was no church altar involved. No musicians. Not even an audience. Just a room of mangled peers.

Seth's mind rummaged through a thousand emotions in a split second. He felt lost in his feelings. He couldn't do it for Liz. This was all about what he believed himself now. Did he really believe? He never thought his life would ever depend on it.

Seth cleared his throat.

"Yes," he said quietly, then louder. "Yes. YES! I am. YES!"

"Enjoy the other side, Anderson," replied John, pulling the trigger back.

An explosive shot rang through the room. John's eyes dilated and his body fell to the floor, off Seth's back. David lowered his gun. Seth opened his eyes. He sat up and turned around.

David mumbled something, then pointed the gun at his own head and said, "I wish I could believe."

Seth closed his eyes again. A second shot, echoing into the hallway and down the corridor, could be heard outside the building. Seth heard David's gun hit the ground first, then his body. He started to sob.

The final shot seemed to have been heard everywhere. News cameras were rolling, Maria stopped reporting, radio announcers paused in their commentary. Another shot meant another life. A darkness filled the eyes and hearts of people around the nation. Although it finally seemed over, the heartbreak really had just begun.

CHAPTER 27

DUANNE WEBB WHEELED THE LAST of the sixteen bodies into the "meat locker," a name his coworkers gave the storage unit that held bodies still under investigation. This had been the longest forty-eight hours of his life. Although he was far away from the actual crime scene, he couldn't get it out of his mind. The fact that he had to look over each of the bodies thoroughly was a situation worse than any nightmare he could have ever dreamed up. It was hard to think that the cold, lifeless bodies he was now performing autopsies on had left for school like ordinary kids just two days ago.

He was planning to call his daughter tomorrow. Although she was thousands of miles away, he felt incredibly close to her. Things needed to change between them. He had been an absent father and now would try to regain that place. Every daughter needs a father, divorce or no divorce. He wanted more than ever to be a "dad." Mark Clarabough had asked him if he had any children when he came to identify Liz's body. When he told him about his thirteen-year-old, Mark started to weep. Quietly, almost with regret, he had said, "Make every moment count with her."

Duanne wanted to make every moment count. His train of thought was knocked off its track by a door slamming. The large metal door leading into the work area had been opened. Duanne took off his rubber gloves, tossing them into the trash in a practiced manner.

"Hello?"

No response, although he could hear footsteps in the hallway. "Hello?" he said again.

A woman appeared in the doorway.

"Can I help you?" he muttered. Her face. He recognized her face. "Uh, do you have a pass or authorization? We normally don't allow the press back into the morgue without a pass. This is a tight case and we have to notify all the families first."

The woman tried to speak. Her words came out slowly. "I, I am family. I mean, I have family here."

Duanne looked puzzled. "Who is it that you are looking for?"

"John. John Theisen."

Duanne's stomach dropped. He knew John. In fact, he had just shut the cooler door on his body. "Yes, uh, he hasn't been identified yet. So, you say you're family?"

Judging by her beautiful appearance, Duanne thought she must be an older sister. "Are you his sister?"

"No, sir, I . . . I . . . am his, his mother."

"Oh," Duanne said, kicking himself inside for not

handling the situation well. He could see the pain in her bloodshot eyes. She spoke again.

"I would have been down here earlier, but I just couldn't muster up enough courage to come down."

"I am sorry." Duanne felt completely awkward. He didn't know how to help this woman.

Janet Theisen paused. "Yes, I am too. Very sorry.

The room smelled cleaner and fresher than she had imagined. It was just like she had seen in the movies. A stainless-steel sink, tile floor, odd utensils that were used to pierce the skins of dead, empty individuals that were under investigation without ever knowing it. The echo when she spoke reminded her of a dark cave and a feeling of emptiness. In the few years of news reporting she had done, never had she come this close to a dead body. Never. Now she was just feet away from her very own son. It had always been one thing to report tragedy, but to stand in the midst of it? It felt very awkward to her.

"I've never been here before."

"Is your husband coming?"

Janet sighed. "I don't think so. His father lives out of town. He, uh, won't come. Too much press right now." She paused. "I know what they are saying about me; I've been a reporter long enough."

Duanne didn't know what to say. She was right. The press was talking about what a failure she and Jerry had been. They were digging up old news stories about their pasts. They had even interviewed a few of the members of their former church to find something that they could blame this massacre on. She knew many of the people pointing their fingers at her parenting were probably worse parents with fewer obstacles. Janet sighed; she couldn't have felt more like a failure.

"Well, I don't believe everything I hear."

"Sure. Uh, what do I need to do here? I just want to get this over with."

Duanne walked closer to her, gesturing for her to come into the room. "I just need you to take a look at him and give me a confirmation that this is your son, John Andrew Theisen. Are you ready?"

"Yes," she spoke back quietly.

Duanne walked over to a cooler drawer, putting his hand on the handle.

"Wait. Before we do this, please prepare me. What shape is he in? Will I recognize him?"

"I believe so. He was not shot in the head, just the back of the neck. His face is still intact. I will also have his clothing for you once we decide what funeral home to work with."

"Cremate him. I want to cremate him."

"All right. I can help you make arrangements for that."

Janet was quiet. Her hands were shaking, along with her legs. The fear of the unknown seemed to be eating her alive.

"Are you sure you're ready?"

"Yes."

Duanne pulled on the handle. A cool breeze blew from the fan inside. All Janet could see was a white sheet. She closed her eyes then reopened them.

"Okay, here we go. We'll do this quickly."

Duanne pulled out the stretcher that John's lifeless body was on. He uncovered the sheet, revealing Janet's only son's face. Janet took a deep breath when she saw him. John's eyes were closed, but there wasn't a peaceful look on his face. It looked tormented. She didn't understand.

"Is this your son, ma'am?"

Janet nodded her head, starting to cry. She recognized the flannel shirt that was somewhat shredded around his neck. Janet had given it to him for his birthday, just a few weeks ago.

"Yes, that's him. That's my John." She pushed herself away from the stretcher and turned from John's face. "Please put it back. Put him back!" She was starting to sob now.

It wasn't the first breath of emotion Duanne had seen today. Each family handled it differently. But to be alone to face this tragic moment, that was something Duanne hadn't seen yet. He pushed the stretcher back inside the cooler and shut the door. Janet jumped when it slammed shut.

"I hate to ask for this, Ms. Theisen, but can I get your signature here? Stating this is your son, John."

Duanne led her to a clipboard. He changed the sheet from the previous family that had been there.

"There we go. I'm sorry about this. I'm sure it's the last thing you want to do at a time like this."

Janet picked up the pen, signing the legal form. "No, it's not the last thing. You know what I want to do right now?"

"What?" Duanne said gently, trying to be a friend.

"Die."

Duanne struggled to find something to say. "Uh, would you like me to help you find a counselor or something?" Duanne felt powerless at this point. He really didn't know how to help, but he felt the need to say something.

"No, I'm not crazy," Janet replied, collecting her purse and thoughts. "I'm in shock. How many people did my son murder?"

"Besides your son, the body count is at fifteen. Although we believe that one of those students aided John in the shooting and later killed himself."

"Did John . . . kill himself?"

"Judging from where his bullet wound is at, no. He was shot from behind."

Janet was quiet. She whispered through her tears. "Is there anyone else?"

"No, you were the last."

Janet turned and headed for the door.

"Ah, Ms. Theisen?"

Janet turned, taking a tissue from her purse. Her gaze made it hard for Duanne to speak.

"I guess," Duanne said gently, "for what it's worth, this wasn't your fault."

Janet looked back at Duanne, almost as if to say something. Instead, she turned and walked away. Her heels clicked down the hallway, out the door, and to her car. She would be going home to an empty house tonight.

CHAPTER 28

"I HAVE TO BELIEVE THAT THESE KIDS didn't just die for nothing, but that somehow something good will come from this." Mark Clarabough cleared his tightened throat, wiping a few tears away. "The night before when my daughter, Liz, went to bed we decided to pray together. I was leaving the next morning for Denver and knew I wouldn't see her over the course of the next day. I didn't tell her I was leaving because I planned to be back that same evening. Even still, that night she prayed that God would keep me safe throughout the next day. Liz didn't even know that she was the one who needed to cry out for safety." Mark started to break apart. Bernice tried to give him a comforting look from the front pew of Bethel Community Church, but looking him in the eye at this point would only cause both of them to lose all composure. "But," he continued on, "that was how Liz was. Not a perfect kid, but one who really lived what she believed. I don't know if this is appropriate to say or not at a time like this, but I can't help but wonder what those last few minutes of her life were like. What was she thinking? What was she saying to herself? What was she praying to God? If I knew, maybe that would ease the pain for a while. But we will never really know. Only in eternity will we truly know her final thoughts. Even so, if I know my Liz, I'm sure she was thinking about finishing her life as God would want her to. In fact, I have found myself singing her favorite chorus. I wonder if she sang it before she was shot."

Mark stepped back from the microphone and started to sing, "I could sing of your love forever . . . "

Mark started to sob uncontrollably. Pastor Trevor Clark, Liz's youth pastor, walked up to him, trying to console him in front of the audience of more than fifteen hundred people. CNN, ABC, NBC, CBS, and FOX News were there. Barbara Walters sat close to *Today* talk show host Katie Couric. Dozens of musicians, sports personalities, and a few well-known ministers and televangelists sat in awe at witnessing such a grave sight. Liz's funeral had been one of three that day, and there were twelve left to go. Most of them were separate, due to the different belief systems of the families.

Lincoln's senior jazz band crowded the small stage at the church. They played Liz's favorite song, "Summertime." An empty chair sat in the saxophone section, symbolizing the student who would never return. Although the song was upbeat in rhythm, resembling Liz's love for jazz music, there wasn't a dry eye in the place when it was over.

Liz's coffin sat directly below center stage on the newly built church platform. It was painted a soft white and a dozen roses laid on top of it. Her senior picture, dressed in a beautiful black frame, allowed those who viewed the casket to picture the Liz everyone remembered. Bernice and Mark had made that decision after much careful thought and deliberation. Because her body was under investigation, it was a week before they were able to get control of it to plan any kind of service. Her body was so swollen that the real Liz was hardly recognizable. Her parents wanted the students and loved ones who knew her best to reminisce about her smile after the funeral, not about the shape of her physical features. Bernice had chosen to bury Liz in her prom dress. After a private viewing for the family, Bernice had commented to her sister on how beautiful the outfit was. She was so glad she had picked it up that day. It was a special final memory, though they never got to finish it together. Bernice felt some closure through just being able to see it on her.

Flowers decorated the entire front of the church; flowers from Liz's friends and their parents, flowers from her teachers, and flowers from people all over the United States who may have never met her but were touched by her untimely death. Bernice tried to put the flowers from the people closest to Liz by her casket. Seth had helped Mark pick out the pallbearers to carry her casket, but he felt uneasy about carrying her casket himself. Shoving her body into a black limousine was one of the hardest things he had ever done.

Seth's stomach gurgled when the jazz selection

was over. He had never spoken in public before, not to mention in front of a crowd of fifteen hundred people. His new gray suit and green tie made him look even taller and more slender than he already was. Although the shooting had taken place more than a week ago, the jazz band had sounded murky to him because of the impaired hearing he had acquired after the gunshots. Sometimes all he could hear was ringing and screaming, but mostly it was ringing. The lights dimmed as Seth rose from his seat and stepped forward. A large, white screen was lowered, and the interview of Liz he had made for his philosophy class started to play.

Bernice took a deep breath. She thought this would be easy to watch, but to see Liz's face again, bigger than life, brought the pain of losing her right to the surface. For the students who were in philosophy class that day, seeing it again was torture. Seth smiled when he saw Liz's face. That was just the way he wanted to remember it. You could almost feel the river of tears flowing down through the aisles of the church that day. Making the choice to show the clip had been something Seth had insisted on with Mark and Bernice. They consented after watching it, and after realizing the impact their daughter had on his life.

"Somebody having a bad computer day?"

"Not me," replied a friendly voice from the other

side of the table. Seth kept the camera recording. The lens focused in on Liz.

"I'm standing here with Elizabeth Clarabough. And to whom do I owe this honor?"

"Mr. Danielson. I'm working on my philosophy project."

"So am I."

"You took the easy way. I'm doing actual research."

"This is research!"

"What?"

"I'm researching you!"

Liz blushed.

"So, Liz Clarabough, what do you think the meaning of life is?"

She paused for a moment. "It's simple. I think life is all about what you truly believe."

Seth smiled again.

"Because what you believe forms what you truly are."

Justin's voice could suddenly be heard in the background. "She's gonna get spiritual on us!"

"Justin! Quit. It's true."

Seth focused back on Liz. "So, what is it you believe in then?"

"I believe in living for a cause, because most people won't die for a dream or even a vision. But give them a cause to fight for, and they will be there."

Seth continued to egg her on. "And, would that cause be something like 'save the whales'?"

"No. This is not about whales but about—" Liz

paused. "Well, about Jesus Christ." She smiled into the camera.

The sound of a fire alarm bell filled the room.

Seth turned the camera on himself. "Gotta go!" he said, turning it off.

The image faded to black and the lights came up. His ears were ringing in the silence. Seth squinted his eyes as he stepped onto the platform. He wished the lights had stayed off, so he could speak to the crowd in the dark. Seth noticed his hands were shaking when he set his notes down on the podium.

"Um," Seth spoke into the microphone, clearing his throat, "my name is Seth Anderson. I went to school with Liz. She was in my class, and she was a good friend of mine. A very good friend." He glanced down at Mark and Bernice, who smiled back, reassuring him of their love and support. "I never thought that I would ever have to speak at a funeral. Especially the funeral of someone I really care about. And my classmates, none of us, ever thought we were going to die. Not in our senior year. Not with three weeks of school left. But here I stand. Somehow, I lived." Seth continued on, looking out at the large audience. He didn't feel so afraid anymore. All he could think about was Liz, hoping that she was listening in.

"I did a project for Mr. Danielson's fourth-hour philosophy class entitled, 'What is the meaning of life?' It was a video made up of interviews with the class, one of them being the one you just saw. I have to admit, they confused me, the interviews. I never knew that so many of my classmates didn't understand the meaning of life. And then, I started to realize that I wasn't much different from many of them. I didn't either." Seth cleared his throat again.

"But then I met Liz. And I interviewed her. She talked about believing in a cause. Living for a reason. And, well, that really stuck with me. I couldn't get it out of my mind. I wasn't living for anything. Basically, my life sucked. I just hadn't admitted it to myself. Until I started to think about this cause Liz was talking about. Why would somebody ever give their life over to God? Especially if things in their life weren't always that great. And things for Liz hadn't always been that great. But this cause, Liz was living for it. The more I was around her, the more I wanted what she had. She lived for something bigger than herself. And so, right there, next to her as she died, I gave my life to Christ."

Before Seth could go on any further, the crowd erupted into a thundering applause. Mark and Bernice rose to their feet. Peers were cheering, friends were whistling, and Seth started weeping. The applause lasted for what seemed like an eternity to Seth. He knew he would have a hard time collecting his thoughts. He tried to speak into the microphone again.

"I—I . . . just want to thank you, Liz, for giving to me what I needed most. A relationship with Jesus Christ. Maybe the memory of her life can do that for you, too."

Seth walked off the platform. Big tears were streaming down his face. The crowd erupted into louder applause then. If someone were timing it, they would have noticed that they clapped for more than five minutes, with nothing to make them do it except their own wills and desires. When he reached the bottom of the platform, Bernice and Mark reached out to embrace him. His mother, sitting next to Bernice, stood quietly and reached out in love to her son. Carol Anderson wished her former husband could have been there. This would have been a good day for Seth to know that his father cared. Now he would have to learn to allow others to care about him. Seth held on to his mother for a long time. Although their relationship had been strained because of the past, Seth promised himself that things were going to be different, because you just never know how much time together you really have.

The crowd started to disperse soon after Liz's casket had been loaded into the hearse. Six of Liz's classmates shoved the casket into a long, black Cadillac. The young men climbed into the stretch limousine without speaking a word.

"Mrs. Clarabough," the funeral director said gently into her ear, "we are ready for you."

Bernice was having a hard time getting out of the church lobby. She had a peace about her that radiated wherever she was. Instead of others consoling her, she had spent her time consoling them. Hugs, tears, and memories were shared with her by Liz's friends and other parents. Even a few of the celebrities had shaken her hand, wondering how a mother in this condition could carry herself so well. Bernice was always careful to attribute her strength back to God.

Janet Theisen stood hidden in a nearby corner. She had been watching Bernice from afar throughout the entire funeral. Dressed in black with a black hat and veil that covered her face, Janet had come unnoticed. Her picture had been all over the newspapers and major network news. Many were blaming her. Her friends were shunning her. Not a single person had even considered the fact that her son was dead, too. She'd had John's body cremated shortly after his autopsy.

Her plan to stay disguised had worked. She came into the funeral late and had to stand along the wall in the back of the auditorium. For some reason unknown to her, she had chosen Liz's funeral to attend. Since she hadn't done anything for John, just to see people was refreshing to her. Jerry, John's father, had only called her by phone. Because of the press situation, he didn't want to be seen any more than he already was. He had asked Janet to send him some of John's ashes. A request she would never grant. Janet knew Jerry didn't care, especially with the public statements many of their close friends had been making, about how bitter the divorce had been and how that must have affected John. But for now, just for a few hours, Janet wasn't blaming herself. She knew if she didn't grieve, the power of death would unleash its sting somewhere in the days to come. For today, the tears of loss were a much-needed release.

The room was starting to swelter as the ushers dismissed people row by row. Janet wasn't used to crowded churches. The church she and Jerry had pastored was in a small town, quaint and very traditional. She passed through the foyer and headed for the door. Janet held her head down, hoping that no one would notice she was there. As she reached for the door handle to make her escape, a woman bumped into her.

"Sorry," Janet said quietly.

"Oh, that's all right, sweetheart," the voice echoed back.

Janet looked up briefly before exiting. She felt awkward even having to say a simple "sorry." Her eyes caught a warm glare coming from the heart of Bernice Clarabough. Both women stepped outside the church. A stretch limousine pulled up. The funeral director stepped out and headed in Bernice's direction.

"Here we are, Mrs. Clarabough. We are ready to start the procession. Do you know where Mark is?"

Bernice looked around and then back through the glass doors. "I haven't seen him in over a half hour. I think he was praying with Justin Le's father somewhere. Do you want me to see?"

"No, no," the funeral director said firmly, "we'd never get you out of here then. I'll go look."

Bernice made her way to the limousine door. Liz's older brother, Ryan, was already inside. He stared out the window, still reeling from his sister's death.

He didn't seem to be handling the circumstances like his parents. He had so many questions that had no easy answers.

Janet walked away in the opposite direction from where Bernice was headed. She turned around one more time to glance at the mother of one of the students her son had killed. A cooling breeze blew past her face, providing some relief to her puffy face stained with tears.

"Bernice," ran off her tongue. "Bernice Clarabough." Janet stopped midsentence. She didn't know where that voice had come from. Her heart and her mind were in heavy battle. Somehow, her heart had won the battle, even for a few seconds.

Bernice turned before getting inside the limousine. "Yes? That's me."

Janet froze. What was she doing?

Bernice started to walk over. Janet tried to run, but her feet were nailed to the cement.

"I'm sorry, did you call me? I'm a little out of it today."

Bernice was now standing directly in front of her. Janet started to weep. Bernice noticed her tears.

"Are you all right?"

Janet shook her head. Bernice reached out and put her hand on Janet's shoulder. "What a hard day for all of us," she said gently. "Is there anything I can do for you?"

Janet stood in awe. There was so much love radiating from Bernice's face. Despite the anguish, despite the pain, this grief-stricken woman was beaming with peace. Deep peace. Janet wanted that so badly.

"Forgiveness."

"I'm sorry, I didn't hear you," Bernice said back.

"Forgiveness."

"For what, dear?"

Janet reached up and pulled off her hat and veil. Exposing her face to the sun caused her to squint her eyes.

"Do you know who I am?" she said sadly.

"A million faces. I've seen a million faces in the last few days. Please forgive me for not remembering your name. Are you a parent of one of the students who died with Liz?"

Janet shook her head, the tears flowing like a river now. She wiped them away.

"Oh, I am so sorry," Bernice said, embracing her. "I know, I know."

Janet couldn't believe this. One of the parents of a student her son had shot to death was embracing her. She was terrified at the vulnerable position she had put herself in. At any point and time Bernice could turn on her. She spoke again, softly, in fear. "Uh, you see, I'm one of the parents, but it's not what you think." Bernice just kept embracing her.

"My son. His name. My son's name is . . ."

Bernice held her even tighter.

"John Theisen."

Bernice's grip loosened. She backed up, stepping

away from Janet's body. This was it. Janet could feel the rejection coming.

"You're News 4's anchor?"

"Yes."

Bernice tried to put the pieces together. She was standing face-to-face with the mother of her daughter's killer. It clicked. She remembered seeing Janet's picture on a talk show she had watched yesterday for a few moments.

"I'm sorry, I shouldn't have done this." Janet turned to go, but Bernice held on to her hands even tighter.

Ryan stepped out of the limousine and close to his mother. "C'mon, Mom, you're not Superwoman. Please get in." He studied Janet's face for a moment. His tone indicated that he remembered the talk show also. "Mother, let's go. Get in the limo." He tried to pull her arm, but she pulled back.

There was no longer peace radiating from her eyes. That deep peace had now turned to compassion. Bernice clasped Janet's hands tighter and looked deeply into her eyes. Now tears were streaming down her face.

"I forgive you," she whispered. "You lost a son, too."

Janet took a Kleenex that had been tucked up into her sleeve. She was crying so hard that she couldn't even make out Bernice's face. But her voice, she did hear her warm voice.

"Thank you," Janet managed to whisper.

"No, thank you," Bernice said back warmly.

"What?"

"Thank you for allowing me the chance to forgive."

Janet turned and started to run. Her black high heels clicked against the pavement. She had never experienced that kind of forgiveness, love, power, and peace. Janet had never received it, but even more important, she had never given it. She couldn't get Jerry's face out of her mind. Janet suddenly felt this need to forgive him for all the pain, the hurt and abandonment she had experienced over the last few years. Her hands scrambled through her black purse for the keys to her Lexus. She climbed inside and buried her head on the steering wheel. Although the world would never hear her cries, she knew someone was listening. Someone cared. The kind of forgiveness Bernice gave her could only come from one source, the God she had been running from. She hadn't thought about her relationship with God for years. But Bernice—something about her made Janet think about and even hunger after God once again.

"Oh, God, I need You. I need You!" she screamed inside the vehicle. And He needed her. She had been away for so long. On such a tragic day in the history of America, she had come home. Janet was coming home.

CHAPTER 29

"I JUST GOT WORD. There are no more students left inside Lincoln."

Margaret paused, and then she spoke. "Do they, do they know how many are dead?"

Her supervisor looked down at the ground, shaking his head. "Sixteen. Sixteen lives. What a shame."

There was a strange pause that filled the dispatchers' area. A moment of silence was given for those who had perished. The silence felt awkward but needed, in respect for the lives lost.

"That should settle things down here for a little while," her boss said, breaking the silence. "This has been one long day. I'm ready to go home. I think you are, too."

"Yes, I was just going. Soon, I'll go soon."

"Still waiting for her to call back?"

"Sort of. Well, yes, I guess." She glanced at the clock. "She probably got out, right?"

"I hope so. I really hope so."

Margaret looked at her boss and breathed in deeply. He winked at her and left. She stared at the digital clock on her desk again. The last time she had heard from the girl trapped inside the bathroom had been more than two hours ago. Margaret tapped her pen on the computer screen, wondering if her friend was alive. Their last conversation had caught Margaret off guard. *How could a young girl have such an outlook on life?* she thought to herself. *Not whether or not God is real. But, in my shoes, whether or not God is best ignored. Life is simpler when you live day to day, but it is infinitely more painful to always live in the smallest of moments,* she pondered again. It made her feel inferior to be so much older yet know so little about how to handle the pain of life.

Margaret took her purse from the desk drawer. She took out her wallet and opened it, staring at a picture of a baby girl. She ran her finger across the face of the child's smile. Margaret reached behind the photo and pulled out a newspaper clipping. She opened it up, reading the headline to herself.

"Mother Loses Baby Due to Negligence. Charges Dropped Against Her."

Her eyes followed the headlines as they had done a hundred times before:

PRESCOTT, ARIZONA: Charges were dropped Thursday in a case against a mother, Margaret J. Owens, who was formally charged with child negligence last week after admitting to leaving her infant child alone for two days, causing it to die. In a formal statement from her attorney, Margaret confessed to driving to a friend's house while under the influence of narcotics obtained at a party last Monday evening. Because her dose of the drug was higher than normal, Margaret slept most of the following day and night, returning home Wednesday afternoon. The baby was found dead in its crib. The state coroner's office reported that the child died sometime Tuesday night after a "long fight to stay alive." Ms. Owens, a single mother, withheld comment at Friday's courthouse hearing. She will be under court supervision and in therapy under the state of Arizona's medical system.

Margaret realized this was masochistic, but by never allowing herself peace, it seemed as though she was living out some sort of penance. She was trying to honor her child with her guilt. Margaret stopped reading. A tear fell on top of the yellowed article, soaking through. She folded it up and placed it back behind the picture.

"Well, Casey," she whispered, "I hope we didn't lose another one. If so, will you look for her and tell her 'hello' from me, and that, that at least I tried?" She paused. "We tried."

Margaret sighed, closing the wallet and placing it in her purse. She opened up a drawer under her desk, taking out a tattered piece of paper. Picking up a pencil, she made a mark under the category "Not Known." For more than twenty years she had kept this piece of paper, and many like it, inside her dispatcher desk. She even moved it with her when she took the job in Phoenix after working ten years on the Prescott dispatcher team. Margaret referred to the paper as her penance. Every time she was able to be a part of saving a life somewhere she would mark it down. To date there were 247 marks there. Although the "Not Known" category wasn't far behind, the deceased category only had 75. Every life she could help save seemed to take a piece of the guilt away that she felt for the one she lost. Through the years it had become her way of dealing with the pain, the rejection, the anger. She had never in her life dreamed she would spend her days being a 911 dispatcher. Her dreams as a young woman were far from that. She had always wanted to be a dancer. But the curtain had come down on her dance. The job she had settled for twenty years later still didn't seem to cut through the hurt. But, Margaret reasoned, one life at a time may.

The piece of paper got put back inside the drawer. Margaret pushed her chair in, heading for the exit door. It had been a long day.

"Margaret," a voice called out, "Margaret, don't leave."

Margaret turned around. Molly, new to the dispatcher squad, motioned with her hands for Margaret to come over.

"Just a moment, please," Molly insisted to the person on the other end of the line. She held her hand over the microphone that was connected to an earpiece. "I just got the strangest call. It was from a young girl. Calling from a pay phone at a convenience store across from Lincoln. She said she had an emergency and wanted to talk to only you."

Margaret smiled.

"What do I do?"

"I'll take it. Transfer it over to my station," she said with excitement. Margaret hurried over to her desk, pulling out her chair and putting her headpiece on. Her computer made a buzzing sound.

"911, this is Margaret, what is your emergency?"

There was a pause, then a familiar voice. "You!"

"What?"

"You're my emergency. I knew if I didn't get to talk to you again today, I might never get the chance again."

"You're alive! Thank God, you're alive!"

"Of course I am. I'm one tough cheerleader, you know. They've got me positioned at the bottom of the pyramid every time."

"I'm sure!"

"It's good to talk to you again."

"I feel the same."

"I bet you don't get this attached to all your callers, do you?"

Margaret laughed. "No, not usually. But you, you are special. You're my miracle. I needed a miracle today."

"So did I! I knew those FBI guys were going to come. Sorry my phone battery died out. But I knew I would be safe, because you were helping me. Uh, thanks. Thanks for saving my life."

"You got it. That's why I do my job."

"I think you're pretty good at it."

"Well, thanks."

The girl paused. "Listen, I didn't just call you back to tell you I was alive, but to share with you that He's alive."

"Who? Your friend that was with you?"

"Ah, well, he made it, too. But the guy I'm talking about is Jesus. He's alive. He died for you, but then He rose from the grave just for you."

"Really."

"Yep. So that you could make it through all the hurt that life brings. He's alive for me, too. If it wasn't for Him, I don't know where I would be today. And while I was waiting for the FBI guys to get there, I couldn't stop thinking about you. With what you said about your past and all."

Margaret's throat started to tighten. "Go on."

"I really don't know what you've been through, but by the sound of your voice, it's probably pretty bad. And that is what God sent His Son for. People with big hurts. You know, like you and me."

"Uh-huh." At first Margaret was only humoring the girl, listening out of compassion for this cheerleader who had been through events that you only hear war vets talk about. As she spoke, Margaret found herself being drawn in by the words of her young friend. There was something this girl had—something that Margaret wanted.

"And, rather than being a crutch to lean on, He becomes the very thing that helps you to live again. After my mom died, I wanted to die, too. But Jesus, He taught me to live. That's why I knew I wasn't going to die today because, for some reason, He wanted me to live. Maybe it was to talk to you."

"Maybe."

"So, I was wondering if you would want to have this same Jesus become a part of your life."

Margaret paused. "Well, you see, I am a religious person. I do believe in God. I go to—"

"That's what God told me your emergency was."

"What?"

"That's why I called back. Not because I had an emergency anymore, but because I knew you did. There is something that is holding you back from the relationship God wants to have with you. You believe in God, but you don't know Him."

Margaret started to cry again. She lowered her head so she couldn't be seen in her cubicle. "Why would a God want to have a relationship with someone like me?" she whispered. "I'm not the person you think I am. If you knew my past, you wouldn't have called back."

"God already does."

"What?"

"He knows your past. More than I do, even more than you do. And you know what?"

"What?"

"He sent me today to tell you that He still loves you."

"I've got to go now."

"You sure? Sounds to me like you just want to run away again from whatever the past is. I can't. You can't. So, let's just pray about it."

"You sure are a feisty one."

"Yeah, I know. I'm part of a new generation. We're going to change this world."

"I believe that. You've started with me."

"Then, you'll do it, you'll pray with me?"

"Yes."

"Cool!! Uh, you can close your eyes if you want. But if it looks too weird, just look like you're talking to someone. I do it all the time."

"Okay. I'm ready." Margaret closed her eyes and put her head down, inside her folded arms, on the desk.

"Dear Jesus," she repeated, "forgive me. I accept You into my life."

Margaret couldn't believe that she was praying this. Nothing would ever be the same after this moment. She believed that. Part of it made her rejoice; part of it made her afraid. She wasn't praying because she was convinced in her mind, but convinced in her heart on this one.

The girl continued, "Please heal the hurt from my past, and help me to understand the purpose You have for my life."

Margaret repeated the words. They were like a healing remedy to her heart.

There was a pause.

"Mom, Mom! I'm in here. I'm right here!" the girl

yelled. It was so loud Margaret pulled the earpiece out of her ear for a moment.

"Oh, sorry. I just found my mom. I've got to go."

"I'm so glad you called."

"Me, too. I mean, that I got to talk to you."

"Hey, before you go, can I ask your name?"

"Oh yeah, it's Angel."

"Angel? Really? Isn't that weird?"

"What?"

"You've been like an angel watching over me today. When you called I was sure that I was supposed to watch over you. But I think God did something very special today."

"I do, too."

"Well, Angel, thank you for talking to me. It was a pleasure getting to know you."

"Yeah, me, too. Well, gotta go. Remember how much God loves you."

"I will. Maybe we could meet sometime."

"Hey, would you want to come watch me cheer?"

"I would love to."

"You know, it's weird. Today has been the worst day of my life. I can't believe I'm smiling when I should be crying. But God has a way of making something good come out of anything."

"He must."

"He does. I'll call back soon."

"Bye."

"Good-bye."

Margaret heard the phone click. She pulled the

receiver out of her ear, setting it down on her desk. She thought again about what Angel had said. The past was gone. She couldn't change it, but she could change today. She opened the drawer that contained the tattered paper she had marked on earlier. Her eyes saw all the marks again. Behind each line was a face, a name she was proud to have had a part of saving. But none of those names could bring her sweet Casey back. Not one. Margaret tore the sheet in half and threw it in the basket under her desk.

"Today," she said, "I'm going to live."

"What?" asked Molly, carrying a Styrofoam coffee cup as she walked by her station.

"Live. I'm so glad I'm alive."

Molly looked at her strangely. "Live? How can you think about living after all the tragedy today?"

"The only thing I can think of is that most of those kids would choose to live if they had another chance. I've got a chance to live. Molly, I'm going to do it."

"What?"

"Live. Live life to the fullest. Why settle for anything else?"

"Sure," Molly said back, puzzled.

"Have a great night, Molly," Margaret said, standing and walking toward the door.

Live. She had chosen to live. Despite the day's deaths, Margaret Owens was leaving her job alive. Alive to face the past, alive to embrace the present, and alive to start a new future. Although she didn't fully understand everything that had happened to her today, something was different. Things seemed clearer. Margaret couldn't explain all the how's and why's, but the questions didn't seem so loud in her head anymore. A deep peace came over her. Margaret knew it had been no accident that she was on duty today. Even more important, she had connected with Angel. And that's what she had been to her, a guardian angel.

CHAPTER 30

LINCOLN HIGH'S BAND raised their instruments into playing position. Daniel Sexton, the school's band teacher, raised his wand, signaling the band to start. The first few notes of "Pomp and Circumstance" signaled Mrs. Levy, the school librarian, to prompt Lincoln's senior class to walk in pairs into the gymnasium. Although it was mid-July and they were in another school's facilities, there was still a spirit of excitement that school was officially over for 543 of them. It was as if there was a collective need, subconscious and unacknowledged, to no longer stare this tragedy directly in the face.

The facilities at Lincoln were still under investigation. Weathered yellow tape still kept most visitors and onlookers away from the building. The parking lot had finally been cleared out, and the shrines that had been built on cars and parking spaces immediately after the shooting were gone now. Only a few faded plastic flowers were scattered along the edges of the parking lot.

The families of those who died had erected a memorial outside the west entrance. They chose that place because it was closest to the classroom where it had all started. Many of the parents still visited the memorial daily, leaving flowers, home-baked cookies, and even a stuffed toy or two. Tracey Danielson left a framed picture of Nick holding little Kasey shortly after she had come home. Life for this community was as normal as it could be. But every day the painful memory still lingered. There wasn't a moment or a second that went by, that someone wasn't thinking about Lincoln High School, scene of the worst school shooting in American history.

The seniors stepped into the gymnasium quietly. A reverence filled the place. Fourteen empty chairs were there representing the students and adults who had died. Although the community refused to accept the two empty chairs that symbolized John and David, the Claraboughs fought to have them there. The community won.

A special section in the front five rows had been saved for the families of the victims. Although David's parents chose to sit there, Janet found a quiet place in the upper left-hand corner of the bleachers. She wore a pair of sunglasses, and she had a friend escort her in and out as quickly as the ceremony started and ended. She never appeared on News 4 again and was in the process of relocating.

Mark Clarabough opened the ceremony with a moment of silence and a prayer, agreed upon by the school board for this particular event. Several choir numbers, a few student testimonies, and a multimedia show of the good times throughout the year made the night seem to move faster than expected.

The teachers had asked that the ceremony be a celebration, rather than a memorial to those seniors
who were not there to share this big day with their
classmates. A large banner decorated the stage with
the words "We Will Survive" embossed on it. That
was the hope of this graduating class. They were
determined to survive the pain, the grief, and the
shock.

The principal, Don Whitiker, got up from his seat
to introduce the senior speaker for commencement.
Both the valedictorian, Liz Clarabough, and the salu-
tatorian, Justin Le, had died in the massacre. Although
Seth wasn't chosen for his grade point average, the
faculty sensed that he should be the one to address the
student body with words of hope. Despite the con-
stant nightmares, occasional shaking fits, and the fear
that he dealt with on a daily basis, hope flowed and
radiated from every word that he spoke. Jesus Christ
had truly transformed his life. Liz would not have recognized him if she met him today.

Mr. Whitiker introduced him. "We have chosen
our senior speaker today for several reasons. Despite
the tragedy we have all endured these past several
months, Seth Anderson has lived with a ray of hope.
This young man is an example to all of us in this
community that we will survive. He has survived.
Would you please help me welcome him this evening
as he comes to speak."

Applause filled the gym. Despite the quiet beginning of the ceremony, it was now loud. Hands and

hearts were united. The student body wasn't clapping for Seth so much as they were for themselves. Survivors. They were surviving.

Seth stepped up to the platform. It reminded him of the funeral for Liz. Except this time there weren't caskets, but graduation gowns, caps, and tassels.

He unfolded two sheets of paper, placing them on the podium. "Fellow classmates, Lincoln student body, friends, and most important, parents of those who were slain in the massacre that took place on our campus two months ago, I welcome you tonight to a celebration."

The crowd erupted in applause again.

"A celebration that we have survived!" Tears filled his eyes. Applause again. Seth waited to move on until the clapping and screaming had died down.

He glanced down at the parents and families of the victims, who sat tightly knit together in the front five rows. "And it is because of you, parents and family members of those we love, that we are here tonight. Your hope and fight to overcome this deep pain have given us a reason to celebrate."

It hadn't been an easy road for any of them. Although they were dressed beautifully tonight, many of them were still reeling from the pain and trying to pick up the shattered pieces of the past. Mark and Bernice had spent time with each of them, sharing about the faith and love that were keeping them sewn together. Yoko, Justin's mother, had attempted suicide shortly after the shooting. That was when the parents had banded together and tried to meet weekly with one another for support. The Les were here tonight, and although things weren't perfect, their faces reflected an ability to rise above the circumstances, despite the pain.

"Our world has become a very dark place. We know of that darkness. We have touched it and watched its actions before our very eyes. But we also know of a hope. Because 'greater is He that is within me than he that is in the world!'"

Screams, cheers, and applause rolled through the gym again. Local news cameras were rolling, newspaper reporters lined the back wall, and even CNN had decided to cover the story of the class that had finally graduated.

Every person in the auditorium knew what Seth was talking about. That greater "He" had been God. And it had been God who had held this small, Southwestern community together. Nobody was going to deny it or stop Seth from speaking about it. If it hadn't been for Jesus Christ, what would have happened to these students and their parents? Prayer meetings were breaking out, fathers were stepping up, and youth groups were coming together. All of this was happening because only God could take such tragedy and find hope in it. Only God could take the ashes of death and despair and form them into beautiful gold. God was the only thing bigger than the circumstance. The media weren't speaking of it, CNN wasn't reporting on it, the newspapers didn't want to write about it, but

God was doing something here. Moving in ways that only He could.

"That doesn't mean," Seth continued, "that things are perfect. Every day we have to deal with this. For some of us, it is every minute. But He is very real, even during those moments when we want to give up. An ever-present help in times of trouble. And God is taking very ordinary students and parents and helping us to live out extraordinary faith in Him. The world someday will no longer remember Lincoln High School as a place of tragedy, but will remember it as a place of triumph. TRIUMPH! TRIUMPH!"

If the sound in that gymnasium could have filled the world, triumph would have been spread to the utter parts of this shadowed earth. Parents, faculty, students, seniors, even Janet Theisen hiding in the back was on her feet. Applause thundered for what seemed like hours. A spirit of joy was rising. Not the kind of joy you just feel, but the kind that knows God really is in control of the situation.

Cameras flashed; genuine smiles and tears filled the hearts and lives of families that night. The parents of the victims stepped in for the sons and daughters who could not be there.

Bernice grabbed Seth's arm after the ceremony, pulling him aside. Peace was radiating from her again. "Seth, I wanted to share a couple things with you."

"Okay," he said back.

"First, I am so proud of you. What a wonderful speech tonight. You said everything I know Liz would have wanted you to! Even more! Really. She would be proud. Mark and I are proud. Thank you for speaking to a community tonight, rather than just a school. This has affected all of us. And you spoke to every heart. Every heart."

Seth smiled. Someone flashed a picture of him and Bernice talking.

"Second, Mark and I wanted to give you this."

She held out a notebook. Seth took it.

"It was Liz's journal. You need it now. It will encourage your faith."

Seth felt a drop of water run down his cheek. He held on to the notebook tightly.

"And I just wanted to say that I am sorry."

"Sorry? For what?"

Bernice took a Kleenex from her purse. "Sorry that I didn't see in you what Liz did. She really believed in you, Seth. I realize now that it went far deeper than the puppy love I was trying to keep her from. She saw Christ in you. And tonight, when you were standing there speaking, I saw what she did. It wasn't you I heard, but Jesus. Suddenly I saw Him. I see Him in you."

Seth looked deep into her eyes. Bernice was right. Christ was living in him. They embraced warmly.

"Happy graduation, Liz," he whispered into her ear.

"Happy graduation, sweetheart," Bernice whispered back.

As Seth left the gymnasium that night, he couldn't help but open the first page of Liz's notebook.

Although the light in the parking lot wasn't bright enough to read everything, there was something she had circled several times that caught his attention. He squinted his eyes, reading and smiling.

". . . But one thing I do, forgetting those things which are behind and reaching forward to those things which are ahead, I press toward the goal for the prize of the upward call of God in Christ Jesus" (Philippians 3:13–14).

ABOUT THE AUTHOR

MARK A. REMPEL (www.markrempel.com) is the author of Thomas Nelson's Extreme Fiction series, including the titles *Point Blank, Breakout,* and *Real.* He is also the author of the upcoming novel *The Waiting,* a modern-day parable about the story of the prodigal son. Mark has been writing, creating, and ministering for more than fourteen years. He recalls making up crazy stories as a kid and then acting them out in front of his family. As he has grown, that desire to touch and see people changed through creative communication has inspired him to dream the dream of creatively capturing the world for Christ.

In an effort to reach people, Mark has been speaking to audiences around the country. After working with hundreds of students at Cross Current Outreach on a weekly basis, Mark has dedicated his life to reaching people through the art of telling parables. He is the author of more than fifteen plays including *The Extra Mile* and *Legacy,* which have been filmed as live stage productions. He has written for *Wireless Age* and *Teen* magazines, Charisma Life, Group Publishing, and has also scripted the recent Bob Carlisle Father's Day Special. He has written several screenplays and wrote and directed the independent film *The Iris.* Mark also took a creative edge in writing and developing the script and story for Treetop Studios / Brentwood Records' three-dimensional animated series entitled *Tails from the Ark*.

As an author and speaker to teens and adults, Mark shares frequently around the United States at conferences, camps, and in junior and senior high schools. His transparent heart, humor, and honest message give him incredible favor with teenagers. He is known by many for his vulnerable and genuine spirit.

Mark and his wife, Brenda, live in Phoenix, Arizona, with their three children— Zion, Azsia, and Ezekiel.

Speaking engagement bookings are available through Brent Gibbs (bgibbs@mitchellartist.com) and the Literary Division of Mitchell Artist Management, 209 10th Ave. S., Suite 214, Nashville, TN 37203.

ACKNOWLEDGMENTS

BRENDA, ZION, AZSIA, AND ZEKE—I love you!

Thank you to the faithful staff and team of individuals I work with every day. Your love and loyalty are appreciated.

The H₂O students—this book was inspired by you!

Vince Brown—you have believed in me from the beginning. This book is as much you as it is me.

Karl Feller, Nathan Goodin, Jason Kruit, Alex Mackenzie, Logan Spillar, Kristen Stuyck, and Stacy Traylor—thank you for your endless dedication visually, artistically, and editorially. No great work happens by itself!

Brent Gibbs—thank you for believing in the vision.

The Extreme for Jesus and Thomas Nelson staffs—you guys are the bomb! God is using you!

Thank you to the many students I have met along the way who have inspired this story. Point-Blank Christianity: simply ordinary people living out extraordinary faith. Let's do it!

Point-Blank was published in association with Brent Gibbs (bgibbs@mitchellartist.com) and the Literary Division of Mitchell Artist Management, 209 10th Ave. S., Suite 214, Nashville, TN 37203.

Check out this chapter from book two
in the Extreme Fiction series,
BREAKOUT

"MS. HARRISON, we have a problem."

Marjorie Harrison, Washington Junior High principal, put down the paperwork she had been working on diligently and looked up at her faithful secretary of five years. "Problem?" she repeated, her long dark hair cascading down over the shoulders of her gray suit. She removed her black-plastic square frames, setting them on a pile of paperwork.

Problems? Marjorie was used to them. Every school principal deals with problems, right? In her eyes, dealing with problems came with the job. Schools have problems, she reasoned with her staff constantly. The goal was to work through them.

"This is an unusual one, though."

Marjorie smiled. Unusual? She had seen her fill of unusual problems. Being the first female principal in the small Roanoke, Virginia, school district brought many obstacles her way. But she was tough.

Tough enough to stand up to a community that didn't always welcome her opinion. "What could be that unusual, Kendra? We've seen it all, right?" She smiled warmly.

"Just come with me. I can't explain it. I'll have to show you."

The two women left Marjorie's big office, heading out of the administration wing toward a small class-room located next to the library.

"Uh, it's been going on since about 7:45 this morn-ing. You know that Bible Club we okayed last month to meet before school?"

"Uh-huh," Marjorie responded.

"Well, I don't know how to explain it. I'm wonder-ing if it is a cover for some kind of cult or drug ring. Whatever it is, the behavior is what I meant by 'unusual.'"

"Behavior?"

The two women turned the hallway corner. The entrance to the library doors was in view.

Next door, a small group of students and teachers were huddled in a circle looking through the glass-paneled door.

"These students won't leave. Some of them are ly-ing on the floor. Donald Rutherland's daughter is crying uncontrollably. And the leader, Jim Smith, is singing songs with a guitar. Marjorie, honestly, it reminds me of when I went to Woodstock in high school. Some-thing so out of the ordinary I can't explain it. I just can't explain it."

The group of students and teachers parted the group so Marjorie could get a front-row glance.

What she saw even she couldn't believe.

Over in a corner amid some moved desks was a student dancing and jumping. She recognized his face. Peter Olmstead. Marjorie had suspended him earlier in the year for selling crack on campus. She wondered if he had been smoking it again. On the ground next to him was Mandy Forsythe. Both her parents had died in a devastating car wreck nine months earlier. She had been on so much medication to deal with the pain of the loss that she had been put in several special education classes just for extreme personal attention. Her eyes were closed. The look of peace on her face transcended any pain that had been there before. One student was praying loudly with his face in his hands; several others were crying what seemed to be tears of joy. The odd thing Marjorie noticed was that although every person was not reacting in the same way, the small group of students all had a look of concrete peace.

"Excuse me," Marjorie said, slipping by a girl who was talking to a friend about how weird everything looked.

"Are they in trouble?" another student asked as Marjorie reached for the door handle.

"I don't know," she responded, confused. "But what I do know is that we are going to get to the bottom of this."

Check Out These Other Groovy Products from Extreme for Jesus™

BIBLES

The Extreme Teen Bible (NKJV)—HC	$24.99	0-7852-0081-9
The Extreme Teen Bible (NKJV)—PB	$19.99	0-7852-0082-7
The Extreme Teen Bible (NKJV)—Black	$39.99	0-7852-5555-9
The Extreme Teen Bible (NKJV)—Purple	$39.99	0-7852-5525-7
The Extreme Teen Bible (NKJV)—Orange	$39.99	0-7852-5678-4
The Gospel of John	$1.50	0-7852-5537-0
Extreme Word Bible—PB	$19.99	0-7852-5732-2
Extreme Word Bible—Black	$39.99	0-7852-5735-7
Extreme Word Bible—Chromium HC	$29.99	0-7852-5733-0
Extreme Word Bible—Blue Snake HC	$29.99	0-7852-5796-9
Extreme Word Bible—USA	$29.99	0-7180-0153-2
The Extreme Teen Bible (NCV)—PB	$19.99	0-7852-5834-5
The Extreme Teen Bible (NCV)—HC	$24.99	0-7852-5835-3
The Extreme Teen Bible (NCV)—Retread	$39.99	0-7180-0063-3
The Extreme Teen Bible (NCV)—Reigncoat	$39.99	0-7180-0062-5

BOOKS

30 Days With Jesus	$7.99	0-7852-6626-5
Breakout	$6.99	0-7852-6547-3

Title	Price	ISBN
Burn	$9.99	0-7852-6746-8
Daily Groove	$9.99	0-7180-0086-2
The Dictionary	$19.99	0-7852-4611-8
Extreme A-Z	$19.99	0-7852-4580-4
Extreme Answers to Extreme Questions	$12.99	0-7852-4594-4
Extreme Encounters	$9.99	0-7852-5657-1
Extreme Faith	$10.99	0-7852-6757-3
Extreme Find it Fast	$2.99	0-7852-4766-1
Extreme Journey	$14.99	0-7852-4595-2
Extreme for Jesus Promise Book	$13.99	0-8499-5606-4
Genuine	$13.99	0-8499-9545-0
God's Promises Rock	$3.99	0-8499-9507-8
Fuel	$12.99	0-7852-6748-4
Point Blank	$6.99	0-7852-6546-5
Real	$6.99	0-7852-6548-1
Sisterhood	$12.99	0-7180-0085-4
Step Off	$19.99	0-7852-4604-5
Unfinished Work	$16.99	0-7852-6630-5
Wait for Me	$13.99	0-7852-7127-9
Walkdawalk	$10.99	0-7852-6747-6
Why So Many Gods?	$16.99	0-7852-4763-7
Xt4J Journal, Plastic Cover	$9.99	0-8499-5710-9
Xt4J Journal, Spiral-bound HC	$9.99	0-8499-9508-6

STACIE○RRICO

You may know Stacie from hearing her #1 song, "Don't Look At Me," or from her touring with Destiny's Child. If you are not familiar, we hope you will take this chance to get to know her by buying her CD, *Genuine.* Or, if you already have it, feel free to pass this info along to a friend.

Stacie also has a new CD in the works, *Say It Again.* Check it out at www.stacieorrico.com where you will also find the latest pictures, merch and tour updates.